MW00625577

A Shawl AND A Violin

Randall L. Hall

Illustrated by Melissa Lowe

Bookcraft
Salt Lake City, Utah

Copyright © 1997 by Randall L. Hall

All rights reserved. No part of this book may be reproduced in any form or by any means without permission in writing from the publisher, Bookcraft, Inc., 2405 W. Orton Circle, West Valley City, Utah 84119.

Bookcraft is a registered trademark of Bookcraft, Inc.

Library of Congress Catalog Card Number: 97-74300

ISBN 1-57008-337-1

Second Printing, 1998

Printed in the United States of America

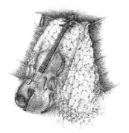

Chapter One

"Careful, careful! If you two break anything you'll be grounded until your missions!"

Catherine, hearing her mother's excited voice, walked quickly towards the living room.

"I'll bet it's pirate treasure," she heard her eight-year-old brother, Anthony, cry enthusiastically.

"And a cutlass," added her twelve-year-old brother, Andrew, dramatically.

"What's a cutlass?"

"A pirate sword."

"A pirate sword?" repeated Anthony, his hopes sky-rocketing.

Catherine stopped in the doorway. At fifteen she was the oldest of five children. She had long honey blonde hair curled at the ends and a passion for horses, for playing the violin, and for taking care of several dozen plants she had growing on almost every desktop, window ledge, and shelf in her room.

A curious sight now had Catherine's attention. There in the living room stood two ancient-looking trunks, each with several woven straps wrapped around it. The larger one was about four feet long and three feet tall, and the smaller one was about two feet long and two feet tall. Catherine could hardly remember seeing her mother quite so excited—although anything to do with family history had a tendency to make her extremely enthusiastic. In fact, Catherine's mother had turned one whole wall in the downstairs family room into a huge pedigree chart. Their family was in the middle, her mother's family tree branching out to one side and her father's to the other. By now there were literally thousands of names on the wall.

"'Dear Pearl,'" Catherine's mother began, sitting on the couch and reading aloud a letter that had accompanied the weather-beaten trunks. "'I trust you are well. Your interest over the years in the family line prompts me to send you these two trunks. They have been in the family for many, many years. As the family on this side of the Atlantic seems to be dying out, I entrust them to you. God bless. Cousin Charlotte. P.S. I'm not sure the contents will prove to be of much value.'"

"Who's Cousin Charlotte?" asked Catherine.

"A distant cousin of mine who lives in England. She mentioned she had some things to send me, but I really wasn't expecting this." She pointed at the two trunks.

Catherine and her brothers undid the straps, and then their mother took a large key from a wrapped packet and tried it in the keyhole of the larger trunk. She wiggled and pushed the key for a few moments; then they heard a click. The lid came up slightly and the children moved closer in anticipation. Carefully Catherine's mother lifted the lid. The scent of years gone by entered the room as the trunk creaked open.

"Books!" Andrew called out, disappointed, as he peered into the half-open trunk. "A bunch of crummy old books!"

"And old clothes," added Anthony, dejected.

Fifteen minutes later the contents of both trunks lay scattered around the room. There were several books, including two old Bibles; some clothing; a few pairs of old shoes; and several broken dolls.

"Sorry, Tony," his mother said consolingly. "It doesn't look like there are any rubies, diamonds, or gold doubloons."

"And no pirate swords," Anthony added dejectedly.

Catherine moved quietly toward the center of the room and picked up the smaller of the trunks. It was heavier than it looked.

"Mom, could I have this?" she asked. "It would go perfectly on that little table at the bottom of my bed."

Her mother paused for a moment to think. "I suppose that would be all right. You'll have to clean it up a bit first."

Catherine nodded. She carried the trunk upstairs to her room, closed the door, and carefully placed the trunk on the little stand at the foot of her bed. Just as she had thought, it fit perfectly.

Taking a damp rag, she carefully cleaned the outside. The trunk was beautifully made, and the dark brown wood glistened as she cleaned the surface. Then she rubbed the metal latch until it shone brightly.

Opening the chest, Catherine smiled as she drew her fingers gently over the cool, deep green velvet lining and traced the edges of the trunk's inside.

She stopped. Pushing slightly on the bottom of the trunk, she had felt the edge give way. Now, noticing a dark green ribbon attached to the edge of the trunk, she lifted it slowly. The bottom of the trunk came up several inches. Feeling her heart beat a little faster she carefully pulled it up all the way.

Catherine gasped with surprise and delight. There,

underneath the trunk's false bottom, was a violin wrapped in a beautifully woven cloth. Carefully Catherine lifted the violin and unwrapped the cloth. The instrument glistened in the light. Reaching for the bow, she felt a sense of excitement race through her heart. She cleaned off the bow, tightened it, and then picked up the violin. Carefully she tuned the instrument, then drew a long note into the stillness of her room. It was warm and full and beautiful. Catherine smiled to herself. She played a few scales, then a few short pieces she was working on for the junior high orchestra. The violin had a rich and mellow tone.

Placing the violin on her pillow, she picked up the cloth it had been wrapped in. It was a beautifully woven shawl. She draped it around her shoulders. It was then she noticed a piece of plain cloth scrolled together and pinned to the shawl. Carefully she unpinned the cloth and unrolled it. On it the words "Christina Cooper 1838" were written out three times.

Catherine sat back against her pillows on her bed and stared at the violin, the shawl, and the trunk. "'Christina Cooper 1838,'" she read aloud thoughtfully, pronouncing it three times in a row just as it was written on the cloth.

Suddenly the air in her bedroom began to shimmer, as if a small mist of water had been sprayed into glistening sunlight all around her.

The next thing Catherine knew she was standing near a stone wall in a country village. Nearby were several small houses with thatched roofs. A shallow stream ran through a meadow just behind them. Several sheep were grazing in a pasture straight ahead, and two men were loading wooden boxes into a wagon pulled by a large black horse. Catherine watched it paw and snort, anxious to move on.

Catherine stood unable to speak. It was as if she had entered a movie set. She stepped toward the stone wall and reached out to touch it. The stones were cool and solid. Catherine leaned against the wall for support, uncomprehending.

From behind her came the sound of humming. She turned around to see a young girl of about her own age walking toward her. Suddenly the girl stopped, staring at Catherine.

Catherine felt chills run up and down her whole body. Except for her coal black hair the girl looked almost exactly like Catherine! The girl walked slowly toward her and reached out her hand to touch Catherine's arm.

"Christina Cooper at your service," she said softly.

Catherine felt her head spinning and she reached out to steady herself. The last thing she remembered was slumping to the ground just before everything went dark.

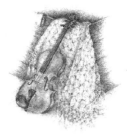

Chapter Two

Opening her eyes, the first thing Catherine saw was her dark-haired look-alike sitting in a wooden chair next to the bed Catherine was lying on.

"Are you feeling quite all right?" Christina Cooper asked softly, concern showing in her eyes.

Catherine sat up and took a deep breath. "I think so."

She looked around the little house. It was sparsely furnished with a few wooden chairs and a small, rough-hewn wooden table. Several shelves held old dishes, cups, and saucers. The room was brightened with some light blue curtains over the small windows.

"Where are you from?" asked Christina.

"Salt Lake City, Utah."

"Utah?" asked Christina, a strange light kindling in her dark eyes. "Where is Utah?"

"You've never heard of Utah?"

Christina shook her head.

"Well," Catherine said, thinking of a way to explain it, "it's in the United States of America."

"America? The New World?"

"Yes."

Christina nodded. "Zion is in America."

Catherine looked wonderingly at Christina. "Yes," she said slowly, "that's true."

Suddenly Christina's eyes went wide and seemed to fill with questions. She reached out and gently touched the edge of the shawl. "Where did you get this shawl?" she asked quietly.

"In an old trunk that was sent to my mother. It was wrapped very neatly around a violin."

Slowly Christina got up and walked into another room. She came back holding a violin.

Catherine looked intently at the instrument. She gasped and felt goose bumps rise immediately on her arms and on the back of her neck. *Isn't that the same violin that came wrapped in the shawl?* she asked herself; *the one I was playing just a few moments ago?*

Christina brought the instrument to her chin and began to play a haunting melody that sang of air and clouds and stars and all eternity. Catherine sat up straight as she listened. Then she reached out and touched the quilt she was sitting on, rubbing her fingers on the rough cloth, wondering whether it was all part of a dream.

"Where are we?" asked Catherine, hardly recognizing the sound of her own voice.

"Chatburn."

"Chatburn?"

"Yes. Chatburn, England."

Catherine knew what she wanted to ask next, but she paused. "What year . . ." She hesitated. "What year is this?"

"The year of our Lord eighteen hundred and thirty-eight," Christina Cooper replied matter-of-factly, a slight smile on her lips.

Catherine opened her mouth to say something, but no sound came.

The first thing Catherine saw was her dark-haired look-alike
sitting in a wooden chair next to the bed.

Christina put the violin down and looked intently at Catherine, her eyes clear and bright. Suddenly she clapped her hands together. "You are from another time, are you not?"

"Yes. Nineteen ninety-seven."

"Nineteen hundred and ninety-seven?" Christina asked incredulously.

Catherine nodded. "Yes."

Christina gasped. "Over a hundred and fifty years." Sitting back down on the wooden chair, she stared at Catherine for a long time.

Catherine sat bewildered. "How can it possibly be eighteen thirty-eight?"

"Weren't you wearing the shawl, and did you not say my name aloud three times in a row?"

Catherine thought for just a few moments. "Yes," she responded warily. "But how . . . ?" She stopped in mid-sentence. "You mean . . . ?" She paused again. "The shawl?"

"Yes."

Catherine stood up and steadied herself near a small table.

"The family will be coming home soon," Christina said, looking out the window at the descending sun.

Catherine shook her head in amazement.

"Maybe I ought to go," Catherine said softly, "and then come back for another visit." She almost felt ridiculous at even suggesting the possibility.

"Yes, please do," Christina said earnestly, looking at Catherine with questioning eyes. "Promise me that you will."

"I promise." Then she stopped short, panicking. "But how do I get home?"

"With the shawl about your shoulders just repeat your own name and the year three times aloud."

"Are you sure it'll work?"

"It has for me," Christina said reassuringly.

Catherine wrapped the shawl a little tighter around her shoulders. "Well, here goes nothing." Catherine took a deep breath, then shook her head. This was so weird!

"Catherine Carter 1997, Catherine Carter 1997, Catherine Carter 1997." Suddenly the air around her began to shimmer with brightness. Then there she was, standing in her own bedroom. She reached out and touched the bed. She was home, all right. And there was the shawl around her shoulders and the violin on the bed. *Was it a dream?* she wondered. It had certainly seemed real enough. She looked at the clock. No time had passed at all.

"Catherine? Catherine?" Her mother's voice was coming up the stairwell.

"Up here, Mother," she called back.

"Time to come down and help get supper ready."

"Okay," she responded, still unsure of what had just happened.

Catherine walked down the stairs, steadying herself with the handrail. As she walked past the living room she noted that there on the table and couch were spread the books and other items that had been in the two trunks. How odd it all seemed!

Christina showed the shawl and the violin to her mother while the two of them put together a green salad for the evening's meal, but she said nothing about the rest of her experience.

All through supper Catherine had a hard time thinking of anything but the dark-haired girl she had met, or at least thought she had met, named Christina Cooper.

Suddenly, with a bite of lasagna halfway to her mouth, she stopped. Almost dropping her fork on her plate, she pushed herself away from the table and headed quickly toward the basement stairs.

"Catherine?" her father called after her.

"Just a second," she called back over her shoulder.

Racing down the stairs two or three at a time, she jumped the last five in one leap, caught herself from falling, then stood upright in front of the family history wall. Her eyes moved quickly up and down, then froze. There, under the names of William Cooper and Lavina Smith, were listed four children, the oldest being Christina Cooper. And in parentheses after her name was listed her year of birth: 1824. Catherine felt her whole body shaking with excitement.

Up the stairs she went, almost as fast as she had come down. She raced past the kitchen, heading towards her bedroom.

"Catherine!" she heard her father call out again.

"Just a minute!" she called back, grabbing the stair rail and whirling around it as she headed up the stairs to her room. Once inside, she locked the door, placed the shawl around her shoulders, and picked up the paper lying on her bed. "Christina Cooper 1838," she said slowly, hesitating. "Christina Cooper 1838," she said a second time. Then she stopped. Did she dare pronounce those words a third time? She had promised she would come back, she was excited to go back (if there really was anywhere to go back to, she thought to herself). But what would happen if her father or mother were to follow her upstairs, wondering what she was up to? That was something she couldn't risk. *I'd better wait,* she thought. She walked slowly back down the stairs to the kitchen and sat down in her place.

"And what, may I ask," said Catherine's mother, "was all that running hither, thither, and yon about?"

"Nothing."

Andrew laughed. Tony rolled his eyes. Her two younger sisters, Audrey and Adrienne, just giggled.

"Nothing?" her father asked, raising his eyebrows as part of an exaggerated look of unbelief. "Nothing?"

"Well," said Catherine, "I'm not even sure I could explain it."

"Sisters are so weird," Andrew said, looking over at Tony, who nodded his head in agreement.

"Only some of them," added Audrey.

Catherine only smiled.

Chapter Three

When supper was finished and the dishes were washed, Catherine headed once again up the stairs to her room. She moved casually, trying not to look as if she was doing anything out of the ordinary; but she could feel her heart pounding as she carefully closed the door to her room. She walked over to the bed, picked up the shawl, and wrapped it around her shoulders. Taking a deep breath, she repeated the words three times: Christina Cooper 1838. There it was, the shimmering in the air. Again she stood just outside the home she had visited earlier. *It is real,* she admitted to herself, *and if it is, then I will find Christina Cooper in that house again. Will she remember me?*

Catherine knocked. There was no response, so she knocked louder and harder. Slowly the door swung open to reveal an entire family seated around the small wooden table. She watched them for a few moments.

"Oh," said a woman, turning towards the door, "there's that door again."

"I must take the time this week to repair it," said the bearded man sitting next to her. Apparently he was in his late thirties, with a pleasant eye and a deep voice. The family went back to their eating, and Catherine stood wondering what she should do next. Then Christina looked towards her. Her eyes grew large with surprise; then a grin spread across her face.

"Excuse me," she said, getting up hastily from the table.

"Christina, you've not finished your meal." The deep voice was kind but carried the weight of authority with it. Catherine watched as Christina looked down at her plate, then back at Catherine, then at her father.

"Yes, sir," she said, and turning she motioned to Catherine with her hands as if to say, wait just a minute.

Catherine looked closer at the man. It must be William Cooper, she thought, the first person in her mother's family to join the Church. Excited, she tried to get a good look at him, but she could see only from the side. What would it be like, she wondered, to have actually chosen to believe someone's preaching enough to be baptized and then take your family across the ocean to a new country?

"Jeremiah, would you please close the door. The breeze is just a little cool for my liking this evening."

The voice was that of the mother. It sounded gentle and a little tired.

A boy who looked to be about eleven years old got up dutifully and closed the door.

Catherine stood there outside the door, confused for several seconds. But turning around she viewed the scene. In this small village, people were walking here and there. Houses, placed at irregular intervals, were linked together by dusty roads and paths. Several stone walls were to be seen. The grass was green and bright. Altogether it was a quiet and peaceful scene, and she listened for a few moments to the sound of birds and the rather strange-sounding talk of the people.

Suddenly the door to the home burst open and out rushed Christina. She ran up to Catherine, then stopped and grabbed her by the hands. "You really did come back, and I was not dreaming after all," she said in a voice filled with emotion.

"Perhaps we're both dreaming," Catherine said.

They both laughed.

"It is most amazing," Christina said, shaking her head.

Catherine nodded agreement.

They stood there in silence for several seconds, just looking at each other, neither one knowing quite what to say.

"Is that your family?" asked Catherine, thinking even as she asked it that it was a stupid question.

"Yes," replied Christina.

"And your father is William Cooper?"

"Yes."

"And you were born in 1824?"

"Yes."

Catherine felt herself going faint again. How unreal it all was!

"And how do you know all these things?" Christina asked.

Catherine took a deep breath and shook her head. She hardly dared to say it. "Well, it's because you're my great-great-great grandmother."

Christina stared at Catherine for a long time, then nodded her head. "I suppose that has to be so," she said, a tear coming to her eye. She stepped forward and hugged Catherine.

"Would it be possible to meet your family?" Catherine asked.

Christina shook her head slowly. "I don't think so. It

seems that only the person whose name you say three times can even see you."

"Oh," responded Catherine, feeling disappointed and confused.

She looked down at the shawl, then held it up in the light. "This certainly is an amazing shawl," she said.

"It was made by Grammy Smith," Christina said. "In fact, her name was Catherine, like yours. She was born in 1742, married in 1760, and had my grandmother when she was thirty-one in 1773. It was during her confinement with Grammy Adams that she knit this shawl. I found out about the shawl by accident, when I was visiting Grammy Adams."

"What was her name again, and the year she made the shawl?"

"Catherine Smith, 1772."

They both stood silent for several minutes.

"What about the trunk and the violin?" Catherine blurted out impulsively. "Who made them?"

"Grammy Smith's husband, John, was a painter and a glazier. He made the trunk, and my great-grandfather on my mother's side, Giuseppe Viotti, made the violin. He lived in Cremona, Italy. The violin was made in 1707."

Back in her own home and own time, late that night Catherine tiptoed down the two flights of stairs and clicked on the light in the large family room. There she stood staring at the family history wall. The names suddenly seemed different than ever before. It was as if they were people. She thought of Christina, of William Cooper, of Grammy Smith, the violin, and the trunk. A great love swept into her heart for this family she belonged to.

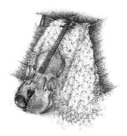

Chapter Four

Early the next morning Catherine walked down the stairs, rubbing her sleepy eyes. It had been hard to fall asleep the night before, and much earlier than she would have wished she had been awakened by her brothers pillow-fighting down the hallway. She stopped at the bottom of the stairs. There was her mother already up and dressed and looking carefully through some of the old books from the trunks that were still spread all over the living room.

She looked up and smiled. "Good morning, Catherine."

"I suppose," Catherine responded none too cheerily. "I could have used a couple more hours of sleep. Can't you keep those two quiet up there?"

"Just sounded like normal life to me," her mother replied with a wink.

"Normal life, huh?" Catherine repeated. All at once she remembered the shawl, the violin, and Christina, and her thoughts tumbled together. She felt her heart beating quickly and she laughed. "Normal life," she said again, shaking her head in wonder.

"Look at this, Catherine," her mother said, holding up an old Bible. She pointed to a page with names and dates printed neatly. "There's some information here I didn't have before."

Catherine walked over and looked at the Bible. It looked very familiar.

"See?" her mother said, pointing at a page. "William Cooper had five children, not four like we've always thought, and the youngest one's name I can't quite make out. Is that John or James?"

"I can't tell for sure," Catherine said, thinking back about Christina's family whom she had seen through the door. "But I'll bet it's a girl, not a boy."

"Oh, you think so, do you?" asked her mother playfully.

"Yes," Catherine said solemnly, with a smile in her eyes. "And if I'm right, then no dishes for a week."

"And if you're wrong, then dishes every night for two weeks?" her mother asked with a challenge in her voice.

"Sounds like a good deal to me."

Her mother smiled and shrugged her shoulders, then turned back to sorting through items she had removed from the trunks.

"There's quite a few things here from William Cooper's family up to about 1840, then there seems to be nothing after that. They obviously left the trunk behind when they came to America, although I can't figure out why they didn't take some of this stuff with them."

Back in her room, Catherine picked up the violin and began to play. It certainly was a beautiful violin, and the sound was clear and pure and rich. She had taken it to school, and her orchestra teacher had recommended that a professor of violin at the university look at it.

"Thousands of dollars is what you would pay to purchase such a violin today," the professor had said, obviously impressed. "Now, how did you say you got this, in an old trunk?"

"Yes."

"Judging from its shape and sound, this violin was probably made in Italy over two hundred years ago."

"In Cremona, perhaps?" Catherine asked innocently.

The professor had glanced sharply at her. "Why, yes, it could easily have been Cremona."

Her parents gave her a questioning look but Catherine just smiled. *Good old Giuseppe Viotti would be amazed at how much his handiwork was selling for almost three hundred years later,* she thought.

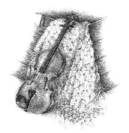

Chapter Five

That evening Catherine took the shawl carefully from her drawer and laid it on her bed. Then she washed her face, brushed her hair, and placed the shawl around her shoulders.

"Catherine?"

It was her father's voice. *Oh no,* she thought, imagining him saying something like "Would you come and help fix supper?" *Maybe I can just say I'm fasting,* she thought.

"Catherine?"

Fearing the worst, Catherine slowly opened her door and called out, "Yes, Dad?"

"We're going to the library for a little while. Would you like to come?"

"No, thanks," she called back, her shoulders relaxing in relief.

She heard the front door close, then the car start up and pull out of the driveway. *At last,* she thought, *peace and quiet.*

"Christina Cooper 1840, Christina Cooper 1840, Christina Cooper 1840," she said softly. The air shimmered, and in an instant she was in a crowd of people who were pushing and shoving and shouting. A light

Crowds of people were making their way to and from
the docks, some walking together in groups carrying large
trunks like the ones her mother had received.

mist was in the air, the sky was overcast, and she could smell the sea.

Catherine panicked slightly as she made her way through the crowd. "Christina?" she called out. "Christina?"

There was no reply. Gradually she came to realize that the people around her couldn't see her or hear her. Suddenly she felt very alone. She took a deep breath and stopped. *Christina has to be here somewhere,* she said to herself, trying to be calm.

She stopped and looked around her. Ahead of her was a large river, bigger than any she had seen in her life. The water was a dull gray, and several large sailing ships nestled in against the docks. Tall brick buildings behind her were darkened with soot, and crowds of people were making their way to and from the docks, some walking together in groups carrying large trunks like the ones her mother had received, some riding in horse-drawn wagons, others pushing large carts. Again Catherine felt as if she had just stepped into a picture in her history book.

It was cloudy but the wind was not too cold. Scrambling up on a large barrel, Catherine looked intently for Christina. Suddenly she saw her standing about fifty yards away with her family.

She looks older, Catherine thought, realizing that Christina would now be sixteen, not fourteen. Catherine called out to her, but she realized she could not be heard above all the noise and commotion of the crowd. Jumping down from the barrel, she made her way as quickly as she could through the throngs of people to where the Cooper family stood.

As Catherine came towards them she could hear William Cooper's deep voice, loud and anxious.

"Who saw her last?"

"She was with me until that black carriage came by and almost knocked us over," said James, her twelve-year-old brother.

"I think I remember seeing her near that corner over there," Lavina Cooper said, pointing to the north, and with her voice full of anguish, "when you went into the office to confirm our passage. We were all standing together and then . . ." Her barely audible voice trailed away into sadness.

Catherine looked quickly around. There were Christina, James, Jeremiah, and Oliver, but no Joan, their seven-year-old sister.

"We must find her," said William, his voice filling with energy and concern. "It will be dark soon, and I fear the rain will only get worse. Lavina, you go to where you last saw her and take Oliver with you. I'll walk down by the river. James, you and Jeremiah walk through the offices over there, and Christina, look where that ship is loading. We'll meet over by that statue at half past five."

Hurriedly the family scattered. Catherine followed Christina and tapped her on the arm. Christina turned quickly. "Jo . . . ?" she asked hopefully, then noticed it was not her little sister. "Oh, Catherine," she said with mingled relief and anguish, "it's you. We've lost Joan. You remember her, don't you?"

"Yes," Catherine responded, "about this high, with short black hair?"

"Yes."

"I'll help you look for her."

Together the two girls moved quickly toward the dock where a ship was loading.

"Where are we?" Catherine asked.

"In Liverpool."

"Why?"

"We've booked passage to sail for America tomorrow with a group of Saints."

Half an hour later the family stood in the increasing rain near the statue.

"No one's seen her?" called William's voice from the dusky, rain-filled dock.

"No," Lavina responded in a voice quivering with emotion.

"I'm sure she'll be found, Mother," Christina said, trying to comfort her. "We must have faith in the Lord. He will help us get to Zion. All of us."

They looked around. Almost everyone was gone now, and the rain continued to fall, even harder than before.

William stepped forward and held his wife close. "Have faith, Lavina, have faith."

His wife nodded. "I'm trying."

"We must go back to our lodgings and get everyone dry, then I'll go out again until I find her."

Half an hour later the family entered the single room they had rented for the night. It was small and dirty and had several leaks in the roof. William Cooper took a piece of paper from his pocket.

"Here's the list of our family who booked with passage aboard the *New Hope*. Lavina, would you put that in the Bible, please?"

Lavina Cooper took the piece of paper, glanced at it briefly. "The list is complete," she said, "but the family's not." She folded the paper several times, then tucked it carefully inside the Bible.

"Let's kneel down and pray and then I'll go out again and find her," William said confidently.

"Dear God," William began, his voice shaking with emotion. "Please help us find our dearest Joan. Watch over and protect her until we do. We set sail for Zion tomorrow, if thou art willing."

Then he stood slowly, put his coat and hat on, and went out into the darkness and the rain.

Several hours later William had still not returned. Lavina sang to Oliver as he lay on a makeshift bed in a corner.

> Hush-a-bye, don't you cry,
> Go to sleep my little baby.
> When you wake, you shall have
> All the pretty little horses.
> Blacks and bays, dapples and grays,
> Coach and six white horses.
> Hush-a-bye, don't you cry,
> Go to sleep my little baby.
> When you wake, you shall have
> Cake and all the pretty little horses.

Soon Oliver, James, and Jeremiah had fallen asleep.

"Mother," Christina said, touching her mother's arm. Lavina turned slowly from looking out the window. Her eyes were red and filled with tears. "I'm going out looking for Joan."

Lavina shook her head. "No, Christina. It's unsafe, and then we'd just have two of you to worry about and look for."

"But I can't just sit here and do nothing!"

"Pray in your heart for your sister and your father. The Lord can do more to help her than we can right now. I know it's hard; I'm trying to replace my own fear with faith. You can do the same. And then try and get some rest."

Catherine had been sitting next to Christina, unseen, sensing the great sorrow and concern that Christina and the others felt. Suddenly she brightened and sat up straight in her chair. "Christina!" she said excitedly. "I think I can find Joan."

Christina turned around and looked at her quizzically. Then she walked toward her and asked softly. "How?"

"I'll be back," said Catherine, smiling. "Just wait here."

Catherine stood up, wrapping the shawl around her shoulders tightly. It felt warm and comforting. "Joan Cooper 1840, Joan Cooper 1840, Joan Cooper 1840," she said distinctly.

The air shimmered and Catherine was in the dark of night, feeling the rain falling hard upon her. It was colder now, and for a few moments she wished she hadn't been so brave, but the thought of Joan focused her attention on her search. Joan should be somewhere nearby.

Gradually Catherine's eyes adjusted to the darkness. She was back at the edge of the dock area. She pulled the shawl tighter around her. The rain was falling faster now and getting colder. Catherine looked around for some shelter. About thirty feet away she spied a small fruit seller's stall. She ran towards it and leaned back against the wall out of the rain. Suddenly something moved at her feet. Catherine tried to scream, but no sound came.

Then, looking down, she noticed the small form of Joan, wrapped in her coat, looking cold and wet in the corner. Catherine reached down and shook her.

"Joan, Joan," she whispered, shaking her gently.

Joan opened her eyes, saw Catherine, and opened them wider in fear.

Catherine put her finger to her lips. "Shhh," she said

reassuringly. "Don't be afraid, Joan. I've come to help you find your family. Your father's out looking for you now."

Joan began to cry softly. "Where's my mother?"

"Come with me. I'll help you find her." She helped Joan to her feet. "You're soaking wet."

Catherine took off her shawl. Wrapping it around Joan, she took the little girl's hand and headed into the darkness.

Five minutes later Catherine realized she was lost, without a clue as to where she was going.

"Where's my mother?" Joan asked as they stopped on a corner.

Suddenly two men turned the corner and staggered towards them.

"Would ya look at that little lady?" one of them said, leaning against the wall of a building to keep from falling over.

They're drunk, thought Catherine, suddenly afraid for Joan.

"Where's your ma?" the other one asked, looking narrowly at Joan and walking towards her, "or ain't you got no ma?"

"Come to Daddy," said the other, reaching out his arms and walking toward her.

Joan stood rigid, petrified with fear. Catherine could feel her starting to cry. She knew the men couldn't see her. *What can I do?* she wondered anxiously. As the men came closer an idea came into her mind. *I hope this works,* she said to herself.

She reached down and took the shawl from Joan's shoulders and placed it on her own, then lifted the young girl into her arms. "William Cooper 1840, William Cooper 1840, William Cooper 1840," she said as fast as she could.

The dark air shimmered. *Oh, good,* Catherine thought as she saw the darkness condense around them. When she could see again she was still holding Joan and they were standing under a street lamp. Her eyes adjusted to the somewhat brighter light, and she saw someone walking quickly down the other side of the street.

She couldn't tell for sure if it was William, but she couldn't see anyone else.

"Mr. Cooper!" she called out into the misty darkness, hoping for the best. "Mr. Cooper!"

William Cooper stopped and stared intently at her. Suddenly he realized that he was looking at not only a stranger but also his small daughter standing next to her.

"Joan!" he called out, racing towards them. He was wet and cold, but a great relief and gratitude spread over his features as he grabbed his little girl and hugged her tightly. "Oh, Joan, my dearest Joan. Are you well? We've looked for hours. Where were you?" He wept with joy.

Catherine smiled and felt a lump in her throat. She couldn't ever remember feeling more relief and happiness, or more cold and wet.

"I lost Hannah when the horse ran by, and I had to find her," Joan said simply, holding out the rag doll for her father to see. "And then you were all gone away."

William Cooper shook his head. "So it was Hannah, was it?" Then his face went serious. "Joan," he said sternly, "you are never, never to leave the family for any reason, not even for Hannah. Do you understand?"

Joan nodded her head.

"Do you realize we may never have found you again?"

"But Hannah—," she started to say.

Her father interrupted her, "Better Hannah be lost than Joan."

"And you, miss," he said, turning to Catherine, "I don't know how I can ever thank you enough for finding our little one."

Catherine didn't know quite what to say. "You're welcome. I'm just glad we found you."

"It's not safe on such a cold, dreary night for a young woman like yourself to be out."

"I'll be fine, sir," Catherine said with a small curtsy. "Good night." And with that she turned and walked quickly the other way.

"Wait, miss!" she heard William Cooper call out. "Can't we take you home?"

"I can manage, thank you." And then, because she couldn't resist, Catherine added, "And tell Christina hello."

William gave her a quizzical look as Catherine turned again and hurried away. She stopped a few seconds later and turned to see William Cooper carrying Joan the other way.

"Christina Cooper 1840, Christina Cooper 1840, Christina Cooper 1840."

When Catherine came back into the small room in the inn, Lavina Cooper was sitting near the window, still peering intently into the rain-filled darkness, and Christina was sitting next to her, having fallen asleep while leaning against her mother's shoulder.

Catherine sat down on an old trunk in another corner; then suddenly she stood up and looked at the trunk carefully. It looked exactly like the large trunk her mother had received just several days before. Now, if the trunk had come to America with the Coopers, how did her mother get it from somewhere in England? Catherine looked closely again at the trunk. She couldn't be sure, but it certainly seemed to be the same trunk.

Hearing a short, soft cry of excitement, Catherine whirled around in time to see Lavina Cooper stand quickly by the window while cradling the sleeping Christina against her. Christina's eyes opened.

"What is it, Mother?"

"I think it's your father, and Joan!" her mother whispered in a voice filled with hope as she rushed to open the door.

"William, oh, William, how did you ever manage to find her?" she exclaimed while hugging Joan tightly.

William sat down and smiled a weary smile. "It's the strangest thing, Lavina. There was this young woman who couldn't have been much older than our Christina."

Catherine smiled to herself.

"She called out to me from under a street lamp and our Joan was with her."

He sat for a moment; then, while thoughtfully taking off his coat, he continued. "She called me Mr. Cooper. Now, isn't that odd?"

"Joan probably told the girl her name."

William Cooper stopped and stroked his chin. "Yes, you're probably right." He laid his coat down carefully. "But that's not the only strange thing, Lavina," he said slowly, as if remembering. William Cooper looked over at Christina. "She also said to wish Christina a good evening."

Christina opened her eyes wide and shrugged her shoulders.

"Joan must have told her about the family," Lavina said matter-of-factly.

30

"Still, it strikes me as odd," said William. Then he stood, smiled, and came over to his wife and child. "But the important thing is that we have our little Joan back."

Christina looked at Catherine and smiled. There was a great sense of gratitude in the smile. Catherine walked over, placed her hand on Christina's shoulder, patted it twice, and whispered, "Good-bye." Then she said three times softly, "Catherine Carter 1997."

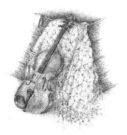

Chapter Six

Catherine walked to the window of her bedroom and looked out. The sun was still shining brightly, and she stood for several minutes just looking at the soft green leaves, new in the trees, and a few daffodils growing in the corner of the yard. April was one of her favorite months, especially a warm April afternoon such as this.

She went downstairs, then outside. She walked into the backyard and sat in the swing. She took a deep breath of air and closed her eyes. Back and forth, back and forth, back and forth she drifted without thinking, feeling the warm air brush against her face.

All of a sudden she jumped to the ground, and walked quickly into the house. In just a couple of minutes she had found the old Bibles that had come in the trunk. She leafed through one, anxiously looking for the piece of paper she felt sure was still there. *Nothing,* she said to herself as she finished examining the book.

She picked up the other Bible and began to turn the pages slowly. She continued to turn the pages without success. Then, in the middle of Isaiah, she found a folded piece of paper. She picked it up, almost afraid to open it. Slowly she undid the crease and laughed briefly to herself. There was the notice of the Cooper family's passage that William had placed in the Bible that night when they returned to their lodging in Liverpool.

The names were all there with their ages. William, Lavina, Christina, James, Jeremiah, Oliver, and Joan. Now she could show her mother that the name that was so difficult to read was Joan, a girl just as she had said.

Catherine smiled secretly, and carefully tucked the piece of paper back into its spot in the Bible. It would be much more exciting for her mother to discover the paper than to have it shown to her.

That evening Catherine sat downstairs reading a book for English class. She fidgeted for several minutes and looked at the clock on the wall. It was almost nine o'clock, and she could still hear her mother upstairs on the telephone. *She'll never get off that phone,* Catherine thought to herself, glancing at the clock again. *And they'll probably call me up in a few minutes to go to bed.* She looked back at her book but had a hard time concentrating. Finally giving up, she slipped her marker into the book, set it on the small table near the couch, and walked over to the family history wall.

Not all of the names listed were direct ancestors like Christina, but they were at least related to her like James, Jeremiah, Oliver, and Joan.

Joan. Somehow her mother had to come down and look in that Bible a little more closely.

"Catherine?" her mother called down the stairs.

"Yes?"

"Isn't it about time to head to bed?"

"Just a few more minutes," she called back up. "I'm looking at some of the stuff in that old trunk."

She knew that comment would pique her mother's interest. Catherine held up an old dress. It looked a lot like the dress Christina had been wearing. She slipped it on over her clothes. It fit a little snugly, but she managed to get into it. She walked over to the window and tried to see her reflection. Yes, she looked like she fit in another century.

"My, don't you look historical?" her mother said, smiling as she came down the last few stairs. "Or is it hysterical?" she added.

"Mother," Catherine said, shaking her head and smiling weakly. "Sometimes I think parents take classes in dumb jokes."

Catherine's mother pulled a face.

Catherine casually picked up the old Bible and looked in the front. "Have you discovered the name of William and Lavina Cooper's fifth child?"

"The one that looks like it starts with a *J?*"

Catherine nodded yes.

"No, not yet. But I think it must be Joshua or Joseph. Those are good biblical names like the other boys' names."

"You mean like Oliver?" Catherine asked innocently.

Her mother pulled another face and shrugged. "Well, I suppose one guess is as good as another."

"I still think it's a girl, with a name like . . ." Catherine paused, knitting her brow together as if in deep thought. "With a name like Joanna or something."

Catherine casually leafed through the Bible. When she had gotten almost to the book of Isaiah, she said, "I sure like this old-time lettering," holding the book out for her mother to see.

"Yes, that is beautiful work," her mother agreed, but she didn't take the book from her daughter.

"I especially like the capital letters at the beginning

of each chapter," Catherine continued, flipping through the pages with her mother looking on.

"Wait!" her mother called out as Catherine thumbed past the spot with the paper stuck in it. "Let me see that." Catherine handed her the book.

Catherine's mother took the paper from the Bible, laid the book down, and carefully opened the paper. She read for several seconds, then looked up at Catherine with a funny look on her face. "Have you seen this paper before?" she asked, looking intently at her daughter.

"What piece of paper?" Catherine asked.

"This one," her mother said, holding the paper in front of Catherine's eyes. "The one that lists the fifth child of William and Lavina Cooper as a girl named Joan."

"Oh, that piece of paper," said Catherine, trying not to burst into laughter. She paused for a few more seconds. "Yes," she said finally, with a smile on her face, "I must admit I have seen that paper before."

"Well, you rascal!" her mother said, shaking her head and sitting down on the couch. "No wonder you were so sure the other child was a daughter."

"And so," Catherine asked mischievously, "no dishes for a week?"

"I suppose not," her mother replied.

Catherine smiled and shrugged.

Her mother laughed. "You've certainly become interested in this family history stuff since those trunks arrived."

"Well," Catherine said seriously, "I think it's because I'm seeing these names as more than names, like they're real people. Do we have any journals from that family?"

"I don't think so," her mother replied. "But you're

right. They were real people. Flesh and blood and spirit, just like us. And someday we'll get to meet them."

"That's true," said Catherine, smiling and nodding, "very true."

Chapter Seven

Catherine sneaked another look at the clock, hoping Mr. Czerny wouldn't notice. If there was one thing her orchestra teacher didn't appreciate, it was students who looked at the clock. "Greatness comes only through concentration," he had said over and over, always in the same tone of voice, "and if you're concentrating you won't even be aware of the passage of time."

Generally that's true, Catherine thought. *I hardly ever look at the clock in here.* Orchestra was one of Catherine's favorite classes because it meant that she could spend that much more time playing the violin, and lately that had become more and more important to her. She loved how the notes translated so quickly into feelings, how she soared, drifted, or danced inside.

The clock read 2:17. *Only 2:17,* she lamented. At this rate she would never get home, never see her room again, and never in her life place Grammy Smith's shawl across her shoulders. She would be stuck forever playing the third and fourth lines of "Fandango Asturiano."

During school she had had this unquenchable desire to get back to Liverpool, to see if the Coopers got off safely to America. She wanted to be a part of the excitement as the family voyaged to the promised land, to

Zion. It had given her a whole new understanding about how the early Saints must have felt to leave their homes and travel across the vast ocean because of what they believed. She had felt so grateful for them, for what they had gone through, and she had decided that she wanted to be there waving as their ship eased away from the dock in Liverpool.

"Catherine, Catherine!" came Mr. Czerny's voice.

"Yes, sir," she stammered, "what?"

"Would you care to join us? or have you already mastered these most difficult lines and are just waiting for the rest of the orchestra to catch up?"

"Sorry," she mumbled, feeling herself turning red. *It's not like it's a criminal offense,* she thought, knowing in her heart that she should have been paying attention.

She stole one more look at the clock. 2:27. *Thirty-three more minutes. I could die in less time than that,* she thought.

Later that afternoon Catherine flung open the front door, dropped her books on the kitchen table, and headed for the stairs. Suddenly she turned around. There in the middle of the table was a note from her mother.

"Catherine," it read, "I've gone to help with Sister Morgan's housework. She's been down in bed again with her pregnancy. Please put a hamburger casserole together. The recipe is here on the table. It shouldn't take too long. Be sure you put it in by 4:30 so supper will be ready on time. Thanks. Love, Mom."

I'll take care of that when I get back from Liverpool, Catherine thought. She started to go upstairs but turned back around. *No, I'd better get it in the oven now,* she said to herself, feeling a sense of duty.

Forty-five minutes later she had the casserole in the oven, had the timer set, and had gone upstairs to change her clothes.

Moments later she was back on the docks at Liverpool. The sky was low and overcast, and the breeze was cooler than she remembered from the day before. Hundreds of people moved around her, some rushing, others moving slowly, many of them carrying trunks and boxes in preparation for an ocean voyage.

She glanced around quickly this time, more confident that she would be able to see Christina and her family. Walking slowly, she kept looking in every direction. Near an office window she saw the family together. William was talking to a man who sat behind a counter.

"But Brother Newsome, our daughter can't travel like this. The ship's captain said he wouldn't take her even if we were willing to take the risk."

With that, Catherine noticed Lavina sitting to one side, holding a tightly wrapped bundle.

Catherine moved through the crowd and stood next to Christina. "Christina, what's the matter?"

"It's Joan," she whispered with a catch of concern in her voice, "she's very ill with chills and a fever and she keeps getting worse. The shipmaster won't refund our passages, even though he admits Joan is too sick to sail."

Catherine turned back to hear what Brother Newsome was telling William. "Brother Cooper, we have two members of the Wilson family looking for passage, that's the best I can do," he said gently. "If we had more time, even another day, I think we could locate others willing to go, but the ship sails in little over an hour."

"I know," said William dejectedly. "But how can we sail?" he asked to no one in particular. "And how can we not sail?"

William paused and looked down for several moments, closing his eyes. "I just don't know if we could ever get the money to go again. We've sold our home. We have nowhere to go. And here"—he motioned around him—"here in Liverpool we'd have to go to a workhouse to survive, if you can call the miserable conditions in this city survival."

"Father," Christina's voice came soft but strong. "Let me stay with Joan. I can nurse her back to health with the help of the Saints here, and we can use the money from selling our two passages to the Wilsons to follow you as soon as she's well."

"Christina," her mother said quickly, "we can't let you do that. I couldn't bear to leave you both here."

"What else can we do?" Christina asked simply. "I'll be all right, and in no time we'll be together again."

Silence fell upon the family. William glanced up at the big clock over the square. They were scheduled to board in less than an hour.

"Lavina," William began slowly. "I think . . ." He stopped and looked around at each member of the family, then reached out and stroked the blanket that Joan lay wrapped in. "I think," he continued, "that Christina should stay and care for Joan, and the rest of the family should sail for Zion."

Catherine watched Lavina grab Christina's hand as tears formed in the mother's eyes. "Oh, Christina, promise me you'll both come to Zion as soon as you can. Promise me," she said almost fiercely.

"I promise, Mother, we'll come together. You'll hardly miss us." Christina's voice was shaking, and she quickly brushed away the tears that threatened to fall.

Catherine felt her own tears coming fast. She

brushed them away and thought to herself, *Things will turn out okay. Things have to turn out okay.*

An hour later all the arrangements had been made. The Wilsons took the two passages left vacant by Christina and Joan and gave the money to Christina. Christina was to live with the Murdocks in Liverpool for several weeks while she nursed Joan back to health, and then the two sisters were to follow the family on to America.

Catherine stood next to Christina and Joan on the dock while fog crept into the city. Slowly they were engulfed by the grayness and could hardly make out the ship as it moved away from the dock. Cries of good-bye could be heard through the increasing fog, then the three of them stood in silence.

Catherine reached over and touched Christina on the arm. Christina turned to her. There were tears in her eyes, and suddenly she began to cry uncontrollably. They held each other for several minutes. Then Catherine followed the two sisters as they slowly made their way through the streets of Liverpool.

Catherine could hardly bear to look at some of the people they passed. Whole families huddled together in doorways, dressed in rags. Small children, shoeless and without coats, begged for a few pence, and there was nothing she could do.

Arriving at the Murdocks', Catherine found a sparsely furnished but warm three-room home. There was a small fire burning in the fireplace, and Sister Murdock hurriedly arranged some blankets near the fire as a resting place for little Joan.

Christina carefully laid her sister on the blankets and uncovered Joan's face. Joan was flushed with fever and shook uncontrollably from chills. Christina cradled her sister's face in her lap and sponged her forehead with the wet rag Sister Murdock handed her.

"There, there, Joan. You're going to be all right," she crooned softly, over and over again.

"Where's Mama?" Joan asked in a hoarse whisper. "Where's Mama?"

"She's not here right now, Joan. But you'll be all right."

"Papa? Where's Papa?" Joan called out, her voice stronger and more urgent.

"You'll see them soon," Christina said as soothingly as she could.

Catherine could tell that Christina was having a difficult time not weeping, and Catherine fought back her own tears. *Why does she have to go through this?* she asked herself. *If only I could bring them home, take them to the hospital or even just the doctor, Joan would be well in just a few days.*

"Christina," she said, "what if I took Joan with me?"

"Where?"

"Home with me. To America, to 1997."

Christina shook her head sadly. "It doesn't work that way," she said. "Those in the past cannot be taken into the future. I have tried several times."

"But maybe . . . ," Catherine said, pausing to think of something, anything that might help. "But maybe you didn't do it right."

"You can attempt it, but I don't think it will work," Christina responded in a voice that betrayed how tired she was.

Catherine sat back, dejected but not convinced.

Ten minutes later Catherine sat watching her two ancestors, whose faces shone in the light of the fire.

Christina's chin rested on her chest as her breathing steadied and she fell asleep. Catherine watched her for a few minutes, then gently stood up.

Placing the shawl over Joan and over her own shoulders, Catherine said quietly to herself, "Catherine Carter 1997, Catherine Carter 1997, Catherine Carter 1997." She saw the air in the room begin to shimmer and felt the joy of hope leap into her heart. Then, suddenly, there she was in her own bedroom, alone. She clenched her hands together and closed her eyes. Christina had been right.

Chapter Eight

The house was quiet. Catherine looked around her room. It seemed so large and warm. There was her bed with a nice, soft mattress, a closet full of clothes and shoes, her mirror and dresser, all her stuffed animals and other paraphernalia. She walked out into the hallway, then stepped to the door of the bathroom. She walked slowly down the stairs, through the living room and dining room, then past her parents' bedroom, the downstairs bathroom, and the laundry room. For a moment she stopped and just looked at the washer and dryer. *What would Christina say about all this?* she wondered, heading toward the kitchen.

She had been a little upset with the thought of the hamburger casserole, canned corn, and tossed salad that were to make up the menu for the evening. But now, thinking of Christina's supper of potato soup and a small piece of bread, everything suddenly seemed quite elegant, quite delicious. Later that night, sitting in the same room as her father, she had said, "This is a great house, Dad, thanks."

He had looked up from reading his paper and tilted his head a little to one side and asked, "What did you say?"

"I said, this is a great house."

He looked at her for a minute. "So," he finally said, "what's the punchline?"

"There's no joke," she said soberly. "I just think this is a great house. Most people never have such a good place to live."

He looked at her rather quizzically, nodded, and said, "That's true."

The next afternoon Catherine's mother was waiting for her after school.

"Anything wrong?" Catherine asked, putting her books on the kitchen table and trying to be calm and act natural. But she could tell by her mother's look that something was up.

"Is anything the matter?" her mother asked.

"Well, from the way you're acting something must be going on."

"Two of your teachers called today."

"Oh?" said Catherine, trying to remember if she'd done anything she shouldn't have done.

"They were concerned, just thought you hadn't been acting yourself these last few days. And . . ." Her mother paused and pointed a big wooden spoon at Catherine. "Come to think of it, that's how you've been acting around here, sort of like your mind was a million miles away or something."

Catherine blushed. *Not quite a million,* she thought, *but at least several thousand.* She shrugged her shoulders.

"Any problems at school?"

"No."

"Would you tell me if there were?"

"Yes."

"But there's no particular thing at school or anywhere else that's bothering you?"

"Nope."

Her mother walked over and gave her a hug. "I hope you're okay, Catherine."

"I am. And you're okay too, Mom," Catherine said, grinning.

"Thanks," her mother replied, trying to smile too.

Back in her room Catherine picked up her violin, playing some of the folk songs and wondering how Joan was doing. One of the melodies seemed very familiar and felt so comforting that tears came into the corners of her eyes. *Isn't that one of the hymns?* she asked herself. She ran down the stairs to the piano and began leafing through the hymnal. She looked for ten frustrating minutes, then turned to the back of the book. There, under "Authors and Composers," she found two hymns labeled "English melody." She turned to both of them and played a few notes of each. *There it is!* she thought excitedly to herself. "If You Could Hie to Kolob." She played through it several times, then read the words to herself:

If you could hie to Kolob
In the twinkling of an eye,
And then continue onward
With that same speed to fly,
Do you think that you could ever,
Through all eternity,
Find out the generation
Where Gods began to be?

Or see the grand beginning,
Where space did not extend?
Or view the last creation,
Where Gods and matter end?

Methinks the Spirit whispers,
"No man has found 'pure space,'
Nor seen the outside curtains,
Where nothing has a place."

The works of God continue,
And worlds and lives abound;
Improvement and progression
Have one eternal round.
There is no end to matter;
There is no end to space;
There is no end to spirit;
There is no end to race.

Catherine sat back for a few minutes and thought
about the words. Somehow they made her feel part of
something huge and wonderful, something that had no
beginning and no end, something that her family would
be a part of forever, and not just her mother and father,
brothers and sisters, but her whole family—Christina,
Joan, and everyone else.

I've got to get back to Liverpool, she thought, lay-
ing down the hymnal and heading back upstairs.

Through the shimmering air she felt herself back in
the Murdocks' house. She looked around for a moment,
orienting herself to her new surroundings. There in the
shadows sat Christina, her arm against the window sill.
It was dark and gray outside, and rain was splashing
against the window panes.

"Christina," she said aloud.

Christina turned and her face brightened momentarily.

"How is Joan?" Catherine asked as she approached.

"She's in the other room," said Christina. "But she's
not feeling much better. Two days ago she was able to

eat but then she got worse again. She's feeling weaker and weaker, and I'm despairing of ever seeing her well again. Perhaps Father should have taken us with him."

"But he couldn't," Catherine responded, "not with Joan as sick as she was."

Christina nodded. "That's true. But now," she continued sadly, "I haven't even enough money for full passage for the two of us. I've given a little to the Murdocks for food—they've been so kind to us—and then we finally called for a doctor. He's come twice, and I had to pay him, and it's not done any good at all. Now what am I to do even if Joan does get better? Send her on alone?"

Tears came to Christina's eyes.

Catherine sat down beside her. "Something will happen, somehow you'll have the money when the time comes," she said, trying to be of comfort.

"Miss Christina, Miss Christina!"

It was Sister Murdock's voice calling excitedly from the outer room.

"In here," Christina responded, trying her best to sound cheerful.

Sister Murdock walked into the room, followed by two men. The first was in his thirties, with sideburns, a slender build, and eyes that seemed to see into eternity. The second was somewhat younger, smooth faced, and smiling.

"These are two missionaries from the Saints, Christina. And Brother Taylor here is one of the Apostles. They've come to give your sister a blessing."

"A blessing?" Christina asked.

"Yes, a blessing, to make her well. These men have the priesthood of God. They can bless your sister to be well."

"If our faith is strong and the Lord is willing," said the younger man.

Christina stood shyly and curtsied briefly. "A pleasure to meet you." Then, thinking of Joan, she said, "My sister's in the other room, resting."

The four of them went into the other room, and Catherine followed. She shook her head in disbelief. *John Taylor! Now this is truly amazing,* she thought, as goose bumps ran up and down her arms.

Joan lay sleeping on the makeshift bed they had arranged that first night. She had deep, dark circles around her eyes, and a flush of redness lingered on her cheek. Catherine could see by her arm that Joan had lost weight and was little more than skin and bone.

"She's only eaten one day in the last six," Christina said. "She seems to be growing weaker each day."

"And the rest of your family has already sailed for Zion, is that correct?" asked Elder Taylor.

"Yes," replied Christina.

"And you stayed to tend your sister?"

"Yes."

"Do you have faith in Christ that she can be healed?"

Christina hesitated. "I *believe* she can be healed," she said fervently. "But I'm not *certain.* I know I need more faith."

Brother Taylor smiled and looked at her tenderly. "My dear, we can all use more faith. What is your sister's full name?"

"Joan Cooper."

"Joan Cooper," the Apostle repeated.

He motioned to the other man, who took out a small container and held it over Joan's head. A small drop of golden liquid fell from the glass vial, and the man placed his hands upon Joan's head. She stirred but remained unconscious as the younger man gave a short prayer.

Then the two men placed their hands upon Joan's head, and a silence settled on the room; but it was more than silence that Catherine felt. She remembered the times her own father had blessed her when she had been sick. She offered a short prayer in her heart. *O Heavenly Father, allow my small faith to be of some help in this blessing.*

When Elder Taylor began speaking, Catherine felt the hair on her arms and on the back of her neck begin to stand on end. The words were spoken simply and quietly, but they came with such power that Catherine felt her heart would overflow.

With the blessing over, Catherine opened her eyes. There were tears in everyone's eyes, and even Joan's eyes were open.

Brother Taylor spoke. "Now then, she'll be fine, and the two of you will make it to Zion at last. Praise be to the Lord, who will take you there. Now we'd best be going. We have a preaching appointment this evening."

"Thank you, sir," said Christina, her eyes wet with tears. "Thanks to both of you."

A short while later Joan sat up and looked around shyly but alertly. "I'm hungry," she said. "Is there anything I could eat?"

Christina laughed with relief.

"Why, certainly," Sister Murdock said, hurrying off toward the other room.

Christina walked over and sat by Joan. "Are you feeling better?"

Joan nodded and reached for the bowl of soup handed her by Sister Murdock. Hardly taking a breath, she finished the soup, then stood up and looked out the window. "Where's Mama and Papa?" she asked.

"On their way to Zion, where they'll wait for us."

Joan sat silent for several seconds, then walked over to Christina and hugged her. "I feel good, Christina, and I love you."

"I love you too," Christina replied, hugging her back.

It was over a month later when Catherine once again draped the shawl around her shoulders in preparation for visiting Christina. She had tried to really concentrate on her school work, hoping that her teachers wouldn't call her parents anymore. The plan had worked, although it had not been easy. Some days she had almost forced herself to think about what she was doing and forget Christina and Joan. But now school was over and she had survived. Her grades had been good, and her teachers had been pleased with her concentration over the last five weeks of school. All of them, that is, except for Mr. Czerny, who continued to look at her as if something was wrong.

"There is something different here," he had said one day. "Maybe it's good, maybe not. But there is something different."

Catherine had merely smiled and nodded.

Now she was free for the summer! Oh, there were her summer violin lessons, lifeguarding at the municipal pool, and the normal goofing off with friends, but at least she didn't have to worry if daydreaming took her attention from time to time.

Sitting on the side of her bed, she held the shawl in her hands. It felt warm and comfortable. She sat for several seconds, thinking about all that had happened.

Well, she thought to herself, *it will be exciting to see Christina.* As she repeated the name and the year 1840 three times she felt the air around her changing.

 Suddenly she was on a dirt roadway. There were beautiful white clouds overhead, and the sun shone intermittently as the clouds moved across the sky. The breeze was pleasant. *This certainly isn't Liverpool,* Catherine thought to herself. She could see no one but a man in a wagon being drawn by two old horses. One horse was brown with a white patch around one eye, and the other, a dull gray color. Neither moved quickly, and the man sat hunched on the seat. Then, as the wagon approached, Catherine could see that seated in the back were Christina and Joan. She thought of calling out to them but realized that Christina couldn't very well call back, so she walked quickly toward the wagon. Christina saw her, waved, and pointed to a place in the wagon where there was a pile of wool. Catherine climbed over the side of the wagon and sat down. They traveled along slowly to the rhythmic jolting of the horses. Every now and then the man would cluck his tongue and yell at the horses, flipping them with a small whip he carried in his hand.

Several miles down the road the man called out. The horses and the wagon stopped.

Christina stood up. "Come, Joan," she said. "We'll walk from here."

Catherine climbed out of the wagon too and looked around. There were no homes that she could see, but there was a fork in the road. The countryside was green with rolling hills, like a postcard of rural England.

The man got off the seat of the wagon and stood with his hand outstretched. "Six shillings," he said shortly.

Christina took a small pouch from the pocket of her cloak.

"Had we not agreed upon two shillings?" she asked, dumping a handful of coins into her palm.

"Six," the man said coldly.

"Six?" Christina asked in a voice filled with shock. "I think not," she returned with rising indignation.

"Six shillings," the man repeated, taking a step forward.

Christina took two coins from her hand and held them out toward the man. He took another step forward, as if to take the coins, then swung his other hand out, hitting Christina's hand and scattering her handful of coins on the ground. The two of them hurriedly fell to the ground, grabbing as quickly as they could the pieces of metal that lay in the roadway. When there were no more to be found the man stood up, holding well beyond six shillings in his hand.

He smiled and tipped his hat. "Good day, miss," he said with mock cheerfulness. "It's been a pleasure doing business with you. God bless you."

Catherine felt anger rising within her. She was helpless and frustrated.

Christina just stood there, her eyes smoldering, realizing there was nothing she could do. "You, sir, are a black spot on the good name of England," she said with force. "And may the extra shillings do you no good."

Joan came up to her and grabbed on to her long skirt. "Are you all right, sister?" she asked.

"Yes," Christina said with determination, as she brushed away several tears. "Yes, I'm all right." She looked down into her hand, then dumped the rest of the contents of the small leather pouch into her hand. She counted the money and sighed deeply. "I'm all right," she said, "but certainly not very rich, not rich enough to get even one of us to Zion."

Catherine accompanied Christina and Joan as they made their way along the roadway that led to Chatburn. Several times Christina had to stop and rest, placing the one small trunk with the violin and a few of their belongings in it on the ground. They had left their large trunk with the Murdocks after the family, in their hurry to board, had forgotten it in Liverpool.

They rounded a corner in the road, and there, a quarter of a mile's distance away, they could see the village. Christina placed the trunk on the ground and stood staring ahead for almost a full minute. Then she sat down on the trunk, put her head in her hands, and wept.

Joan sat down beside her and leaned against her side.

"Don't cry, Christina, it makes me feel sad," she said. "And I think Father would want us to be happy."

Christina tried to smile and wiped her tears with her skirt. "I'm sorry, Joan. I guess I just need to have more faith. And I'm not sure if I'm crying because I'm sad or because I'm glad to see the old village again."

Catherine sat on the other side of Christina with her hand upon her shoulder. She felt a lump in her throat. *Would I have even had the faith to do what she's doing?*

Christina stood up and pulled Joan with her. "Come on," she said, "we only have a little ways to go."

Catherine walked silently beside them. The countryside was clean and fresh and green. Catherine breathed deeply. It was such a relief to get away from the soot and smells of Liverpool. She couldn't understand why anyone would even want to live there.

"It's home!" Joan shouted suddenly. "It's home!"

Joan ran ahead. "Hurry," she said anxiously. "Come on, come on. Hurry up!"

Christina smiled at her sister's excitement. "We're coming. I mean I'm coming," she said, giving Catherine a quick smile. But she wasn't fast enough to satisfy Joan, who came back and started pulling at her skirt.

"Joan," Christina finally said, out of breath, "I can't run and carry this trunk at the same time. You're going to have to be patient."

Quieted, Joan quit urging her sister on for a moment. But then she danced and skipped ahead, waving her arms and encouraging Christina to go as fast as she could.

They came near their old house and Christina stopped, dropping the trunk to the ground. She stared at the house for several seconds, and Catherine could see tears forming in the corners of her eyes.

Joan ran on ahead, up the lane to the house, and started calling, "Mama, Papa. We're home."

"Joan!" Christina called out in alarm, but it was too late. Joan had pushed open the familiar door and disappeared inside.

Christina hesitated just a second, then began running toward the door herself. It was then that Joan backed out of the house with a look of pure bewilderment on her face.

A man with a long gray beard appeared at the doorway and stood silently with his arms folded.

Rushing up to her sister, Christina threw her arms around her and began backing away.

"Excuse us, sir," she said, "my sister is just a little confused."

The man continued to stand in the doorway, saying nothing. Then he turned, went back inside, and closed the door firmly.

"Mama, where's Mama?" Joan asked; then, confused, she started to cry.

"Joan, Joan," Christina said, trying to comfort her sister. She walked her over to a large stone, and the two of them sat down. "Joan, Mama and Papa have gone to America on a ship, they've gone to Zion."

"They're not home?" she asked through her tears.

"No."

"But who's in our house?"

"It's not our house anymore, Joan. Papa sold it before he left for Zion."

"Then where's home?"

Christina took a deep breath. Catherine could see that Christina was doing her best to keep from crying herself. "We're going to Aunt Martha and Uncle Robert's house, to see if they'll take us in."

Joan, still numbed by what had transpired in the last several minutes, walked alongside Christina, clinging to her skirt with a blank stare on her face. Catherine wished she could scoop her up and hold her and tell her that everything would turn out all right.

They walked slowly along the road that wound through the village, across a small stream, and up a slight incline on the other side. Christina stopped and put the trunk down. "There, Joan, see? There's Uncle Robert and Aunt Martha's house."

Joan stared straight ahead and made no sign of recognition.

Picking up the trunk, they continued on for the last two hundred yards. Catherine watched as Christina placed the trunk on the ground and knocked on the door.

She could hear the shuffling of feet inside, and then the door was pulled open.

A woman with light brown hair stood in the doorway,
wiping her hands on her apron. Her eyes widened.
"Christina! Joan!" she exclaimed.

A woman with light brown hair stood in the doorway, wiping her hands on her apron. Her eyes widened. "Christina! Joan!" she exclaimed, rushing out and throwing her arms around the two of them. She hugged them as tightly as she could. Then suddenly she stood up and looked around. "I thought you'd gone to America."

The most Christina could do was shake her head no.

"And where's your folks, darlin'?"

"Gone to Zion."

"But . . . ," Aunt Martha began, confused.

"Joan got sick in Liverpool, very sick with chills and fever, and we were afraid she might die on the voyage, so I stayed to nurse her back to health. We plan to follow them."

"And?"

"We haven't sufficient money," Christina said, looking down at the ground. "We paid for room and board in Liverpool and then for passage here by wagon."

"And the man stole some of our money too, Aunt Martha," Joan piped up.

"Is that true, Christina?"

Christina nodded.

"Such a scoundrel ought to be flogged," continued Aunt Martha, "taking advantage of two young girls like that. He didn't hurt you, did he?" she asked.

Christina shook her head. "No."

There were a few seconds of silence, and then Christina spoke again. "We're needing a place to stay until I can earn enough to secure passage to Zion."

Christina paused and took a breath. She looked down at the ground for several seconds, then looked up and blurted out, "May we stay here? It would only be temporary, and we could help around the place."

58

Catherine could see Christina's muscles go tense as she waited for the reply.

"Why, of course, dear," Aunt Martha said, hugging the two of them again. "Of course. And for as long as you need to."

Catherine watched as Christina crumpled in her aunt's arms, exhausted.

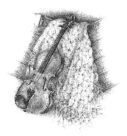

Chapter Nine

Catherine rolled over and looked at the clock on her dresser. 11:07. It hurt just to move. She sat up slowly in bed. This was one of the worst stomachaches she could ever remember. And she had been feeling steadily worse ever since she had gone up to her room a little after seven o'clock.

She got out of bed slowly and went downstairs. The light was still on in the living room, and her father was reading a book. Leaning against the doorway, she said, "Dad?"

Her father looked up. "You all right, Catherine?"

She shook her head no.

He put his book down and walked toward her. He felt her forehead with his hand. "I think you've got a bit of a fever."

"My stomach still hurts."

"Did you take some Pepto-Bismol?"

"Yes."

"It didn't help?"

She shook her head no.

"Well," he said, "I wish your mother were here. She might have a better idea of what's going on. But she called and said she wouldn't be back until late tomorrow night. I guess your Aunt Janette is as excited about those books and two family Bibles as your mother is."

Catherine tried to smile, but it wasn't very convincing.

"Would you like a blessing?"

Catherine nodded yes.

Fifteen minutes later Brother Burton, their home teacher, knocked on the door.

"Come in, Leonard," Catherine's father said. "Thanks for coming."

Brother Burton smiled the kindly smile that was almost always on his face. He was over seventy years old, with white hair and a tall, thin body that was beginning to bend with time. He had been their home teacher for almost five years and had been a part of a number of blessings. Catherine was glad to see him.

"Not feeling shipshape, I understand," he said, reaching out to shake her hand.

Catherine winced and shook her head. "No," she returned softly, trying to smile and be polite.

"Sit here, Catherine," her father said gently, moving a chair into the middle of the room.

Moments later the blessing had been given, and Brother Burton waved good-bye. "Take care now," he said as he smiled reassuringly and closed the door behind him.

Catherine's father carefully helped her upstairs. "Still hurt?" he asked.

She nodded.

"Well, I think you'll be able to get some rest now."

"I hope so," she whispered. "Thanks, Dad."

"You're welcome."

Minutes later she had fallen asleep.

Catherine woke in the morning, feeling the pain again. It was after eight o'clock, but she couldn't hear any sound of movement in the house. Then she remembered. It was Sunday. Her brothers and sisters wouldn't be up for a while yet. Had her dad gone to his meetings? She lay back on her bed, wondering why she hadn't gotten better. Did she have enough faith? She thought of Christina and Joan and wondered how they were doing. Then she saw her door slowly open. Her father peeked in. Seeing her awake, he smiled, opened the door wide, and entered.

"Thought I'd see how you're doing before I headed off to my meetings. Feeling any better?"

"Not much."

He walked over and sat on her bed, reached out, and touched her forehead. "Well, at least your fever is doing well."

She smiled weakly.

"Let me call the doctor before I go."

"It's Sunday."

"Well, I'll call the emergency room at the hospital. Maybe the nurse can tell us something."

A few minutes later her father came back. "They said a twenty-four-hour stomach flu's been going around, so they recommended we wait until this evening and see how you're doing then."

Catherine nodded.

Her father looked at her again for several seconds. "You going to be all right?"

"Sure," she said. "But I sure wish that twenty-four hours would hurry up and get here."

"When was it you started to feel sick last night?"

"It was just a little bit after we ate supper."

"Uh-oh," said her father. "I hope it wasn't that hamburger-rice concoction I cooked up."

"I doubt it," replied Catherine. "No one else has

complained about feeling sick, and Anthony and Andrew ate a ton of that stuff."

Her father nodded, reassured. "Well, we'll check on you in a little while."

Later Catherine sat in the silence of a Sunday afternoon. The rest of her family was at church, and she lay on her bed. The pain was still there but it seemed to have settled in the right side of her stomach. Bored, she decided to go downstairs and look at the genealogy wall. *I wonder what Christina's family did for stomach flu?* she thought as she rolled gently out of bed.

It took her quite a while to get on her feet. And then, approaching the doorway, she felt a sharp pain that doubled her over. She leaned against the wall for what seemed like several minutes and tried to breathe deeply. The pain was still there. She tried to take several more steps but couldn't even stand upright. Slowly, she hobbled back and fell on her bed.

Over an hour later the front door opened, and she heard her brothers bounding up the stairs to change out of their Sunday clothes. Seconds later she heard her father's measured step coming up the stairs. "So?" he asked hopefully as he entered her room.

"It's worse," she whispered. "I can't even stand up straight."

"Let me call the hospital again."

Her father went back downstairs, and Catherine lay back on her bed and said a short prayer.

Moments later he reappeared. "They want to see you right now."

Oh great, she thought, *just what I need.* Then she spoke aloud. "But don't you have a meeting tonight?"

"I'll cancel it. Grab your slippers and I'll help you downstairs."

Catherine woke in the middle of the night. There was no sound, and she had a hard time turning over. She could feel a dull pain where the incision had been made. Appendicitis. And apparently it was lucky they had gone in when they did. The doctor said it hadn't been that far away from rupturing.

Just a trace of light came through the window from the parking lot. Catherine's eyes adjusted to the semi-darkness, and gradually she was able to see. There, in the corner, slumped into a chair, with his feet up on another chair, was her father. He had a hospital blanket covering him, but he didn't look very comfortable. She lay there thinking how glad she was that he was there, even if he was asleep. She thought of Christina, with her own father far across the ocean.

She continued to stare into the grayness of the room. Occasional noises let her know that others were awake on the floor, but for the most part it was quiet.

She thought of her mother—how she loved her family and the Church and genealogy work. She even wondered about sharing her secret with her mother, but somehow it didn't seem like the best thing to do—at least not for now.

She thought of Andrew and Anthony, Audrey and Adrienne, and about how they teased and irritated her sometimes. And she felt bad for the things she occasionally said in return. Funny how you thought about your family in times like this.

The pain increased, and she considered ringing for the nurse to give her some more pain medication. *No, she thought, I don't want to bother anyone, and it's probably not that good for me anyway.* But the pain grew steadily worse. She looked up at the clock on the wall. 1:50. She had been awake for almost an hour now. Turning over, she felt a sharp stab of pain. She let out an involuntary cry of pain.

Her father moved under the blanket, then sat up straight and looked toward Catherine. "Catherine?" he whispered.

"What?"

"You okay?"

"Well, the pain's coming back."

Her father stood up and walked over and sat down on the corner of her bed. He felt her forehead. Then he brushed away her bangs and smiled. "Pretty bad?"

Catherine nodded, fighting back the tears. It was getting quite a bit worse.

"Should I ring for the nurse?"

"Would you give me a blessing first?"

He patted her on the shoulder. "Sure," he said.

Standing up, he bowed his head for just a moment. Then she felt the weight of his hands upon her head.

"Catherine Marie Carter," he began.

When he finished, Catherine lay back down. The pillow felt cool on the back of her neck, and the faint light continued to filter in from the outside.

"Thanks, Dad," she said, feeling drowsy.

Her father smiled and sat next to her, letting his hand rest on her arm. Moments later she was asleep.

The next thing Catherine knew, light was streaming in the window and her mother was sitting next to her.

"Well, it's about time you regained consciousness," her mother said, smiling. "I come all the way home to see you, and you don't even speak to me for hours."

Catherine smiled. "How was your trip?"

"Good, very good." Her mother reached out and placed her hand on Catherine's arm. "How are you feeling?"

"A little sore, but better than I was yesterday, that's for sure. At least I think I'll live."

"Now, there's a comforting thought," her mother said, smiling again. But Catherine could see the concern in her eyes.

"Where's Dad?"

"Home getting some breakfast for the troops. He should be back in just a little while. I think they're going to let us take you home this morning."

Catherine took a deep breath and lay back on the pillow. "It will be good to get home," she said softly.

Chapter Ten

Three days later Catherine sat propped up in bed, writing in her journal. *I wonder what's happened to Christina,* she said half aloud.

She looked around the room at the cards and balloons and gifts her friends had brought. Everyone had really been good to her, and it had helped her realize all the people who actually cared about her. But what about Christina? How was she getting along? And Joan? Catherine was impatient to find out.

She got out of bed carefully, walked across the room, and picked up the shawl lying on her dresser. She could move now with very little pain. She took a deep breath and smiled. *I wonder,* she thought, *what will happen if I mention a particular month and day as well as the year.* "Christina Cooper, April 7, 1841" she began. When the light settled around her Catherine looked this way and that, unable to see Christina at first. But it did seem earlier in the year, more like April than June. *It must work,* she said to herself.

Then she noticed two people sitting on a large rock behind a tree. She heard familiar laughter and walked toward the sound.

She stopped short as she noticed Christina sitting with a young man. He was blonde haired, quite large, and pleasant looking. Catherine could tell immediately that he had some special feelings for Christina. She listened to their hushed tones.

"But, Stewart, there's not a question in my mind but that I have to follow my family to Zion. My heart lets me know that is what I must do."

"And my heart wonders why you should go halfway around the world when there may be happiness for you right here in Chatburn. Aren't there still those of your new faith here?"

"Yes . . ." Christina paused. "But my family is gone, and besides . . ." She paused again. "I have to think of Joan as well. Even if I wanted to stay, what would happen to her? And what would Mama and Papa say?"

"Joan could be happy here too. She has many friends, and this has been her home since birth. And there in Zion, as you call it, she would not know anyone. I think it would be harder for her there."

Christina laughed and shook her head. Then suddenly she became serious again. She paused for several seconds and looked up at the large white clouds that sat in the sky above them. "Still, I'm afraid we may be here longer than I had hoped, for lack of money. It has been nearly ten months now, and I haven't even earned half of what is necessary to secure passage on a ship to America for me, let alone for Joan."

So it is April! Catherine thought, excited about her new discovery.

They sat together for several minutes, then Christina stood up. "I must go now. Aunt Martha will be wondering about me, and," she said, laughing, "about you. And then she'll run right over to your mother, and we'll never hear the end of all this."

"I hope I never see the end of all this," Stewart said seriously.

Christina blushed and started walking down the roadway. Stewart followed, slowly at first, then more rapidly until he caught up with her. "I've tried to understand this new faith, tried to believe. But all this talk of golden bibles and angels—it's hard for a man to accept."

"I'm not asking you to join our faith, Stewart."

"I know. But I thought that, well, I thought that if I did you might be more willing to listen to how I feel about the future."

Christina put her finger to her lips, signaling quiet. "No more talk of the future today."

By this time Catherine could see they were approaching Aunt Martha's home.

"You'd best go, Stewart."

"Can I stop by this evening?"

"Tomorrow."

Stewart smiled wistfully but nodded his head. He reached out and touched her hand, then turned quickly around and headed down the road with long, vigorous strides.

Catherine stepped into the sunlight.

"Christina," she said.

Christina turned around. "Catherine!"

"How are you?"

"Confused."

"What do you mean?"

"Have you been here long?"

"About ten minutes—ever since you were sitting on the rock by that big tree."

"Then you know about Stewart."

"Yes."

"I met him just a few days after returning here. His father owns quite a bit of land in the meadows, and they have a large herd of sheep. I became acquainted with him when I was asked to come and do some house-cleaning while his mother was sick. And he has become more and more persistent."

"I can tell. And I think I can tell how he feels about you," Catherine said, smiling. "But how do you feel about him?"

Christina stood there for several seconds, as if weighing her feelings. "I think I could like him very much, if I would let myself."

"Could you love him?"

"Perhaps."

"Enough to . . ." Catherine stopped here, not wanting to pry into feelings where she didn't belong.

"Perhaps," came Christina's reply to the unfinished question.

The two of them stood together in the gathering darkness.

"He is very kind and very good."

"But he does not believe in the gospel?"

"He believes in Jesus and the Bible, but not the Restoration," Christina said. "But perhaps that would come. He is such a good man, I can't see him being blind to the truth forever."

"But you can't be sure."

"I know."

There was another silence, and Catherine thought she ought to change the subject. "Have you heard anything from your family?"

Christina nodded her head. "Yes, three letters. They are well and anxious for us to join them. The Saints have gathered to a place called Nauvoo." Christina paused. "I miss my family very much."

The two of them walked along in silence. The sun

was moving slowly down the western sky, and the shadows lengthened in front of them. The air was warm and pleasant and fragrant. It was a beautiful evening, full of bird calls and soft breezes. Catherine took a deep breath and let it out slowly, humming softly to herself.

Moments later they stood in front of Christina's Aunt Martha's house.

"Would you like to come in?"

"Isn't anyone home?"

"No. There is a meeting of the Saints tonight at Downham. Some elders from America are preaching and everyone has gone."

"How come you're not there?"

"I was supposed to be home in time to go but . . ." Christina's voice trailed off apologetically.

"But you spent too much time talking with Stewart?" Catherine asked with a little bit of a motherly tone.

"I don't have to go to every meeting," Christina returned, somewhat defensively. "I still have my testimony."

"I know," Catherine said, gently reassuring her friend. "I know." Still, she thought to herself, that wasn't a good sign.

With that, the two of them entered a home that seemed much like Christina's old home, only a bit larger and with a few more comforts.

"Sometimes I'm very confused, and sometimes I'm very lonely," Christina confided, sitting down on a padded hardwood chair near the fireplace.

Catherine nodded her understanding. "I think you're very brave and very strong," she said.

Christina smiled weakly. "I wish I felt brave or strong."

"How's Joan feeling?"

"She's feeling very well."

"So she hasn't been sick anymore?"

"Not since the blessing in Liverpool."

Catherine thought for a moment about the blessing her father had given her in the hospital and how the pain had disappeared and she had been able to sleep through the night. Yet the first blessing hadn't healed her appendix, and she had still had to have the operation. She wasn't exactly sure why Joan would be totally healed and she wouldn't. Did she have sufficient faith? the faith to be healed or to leave a home and travel across an ocean to a new land, even if it was the promised land?

"And when do you plan to go to America?"

"When I have sufficient money."

Catherine could tell from the tone of Christina's voice that she was discouraged.

Christina stood up and walked to the corner of the room, opened the small trunk, and lifted out her violin.

She tuned it for just a moment. "Sometimes this is the one thing that can give me peace and calm me inside. I play the songs my mother and father love, and somehow it makes me feel close to them."

She began to play. She played slowly, carefully. The melodies spoke of longing, separation, and loneliness. Then gradually the feeling shifted to peace and a sense of contentment.

Catherine loved to watch her play. Christina's whole mind and body seemed absorbed in the music, and it was almost as if the violin were a part of her and that her soul and movement brought the music and set it drifting on the air.

After one piece Catherine applauded spontaneously.

Christina blushed and did a small curtsy. Then she

picked up the bow and began again. It was a lively dance tune, and she tapped her foot in time with the music. As a smile crossed Christina's lips Catherine smiled as well and began to clap her hands in time with the music.

Christina finished with a flourish and took several deep breaths. She laughed, and Catherine joined her.

"Here, you play something!"

"Oh, I can't play that well."

"I'm sure you can play very well," said Christina reassuringly, holding the violin out toward Catherine.

Catherine took the violin. *How odd to be playing this here in this house, over a hundred and fifty years before I played it this afternoon!* she thought. She played some short classical pieces and then moved into a good, old-fashioned American hoedown tune. Although she deeply loved classical music, she always loved the energy and enthusiasm of the fiddle tunes. She energetically played three in a row while Christina tapped her foot and clapped her hands. When Catherine stopped, Christina stood up and applauded.

"That's wonderful!" she said enthusiastically. "I fear you play much better than I."

Catherine shook her head. "I don't think so."

"Play one more, and then I'd better do some carding of that wool on the table."

Catherine played a version of "Greensleeves" she had learned, and as she did so, tears came to Christina's eyes. "One of my mother's favorite tunes," she said when Catherine had finished.

Catherine handed the violin to Christina, who took it, then paused. She looked intently at the violin and her face brightened, then went sad.

"What's the matter?"

"Nothing," Christina said pensively, holding up the

violin and looking at it carefully. "What do you suppose someone would pay to buy this violin?"

Catherine shook her head. "I don't know."

"Do you suppose I could get enough for passage to Zion?"

Catherine shrugged and felt a chill in the middle of her stomach. Would Christina really consider selling the violin?

At that moment they heard the sound of singing and footsteps approaching the house.

"Sounds like Aunt Martha, Uncle Robert, and Joan."

"I'd better be going," Catherine said, glancing toward the door.

Christina stepped toward her and took her hand. "Thank you," she said. "I enjoyed this evening so very much. It was a great comfort to me."

"I'm glad," Catherine said. "I enjoyed it too."

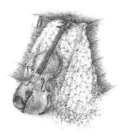

Chapter Eleven

Two weeks later Catherine once again stood in her room, poised to return to England. She decided on a date two months from when she had last visited. In a few moments she was standing in what she soon realized was a small, grassy field behind Aunt Martha's home. Christina was sitting on a stile, and Stewart was standing next to her.

Catherine walked closer, a little nervously. She stopped for a few moments, but Stewart was speaking in low tones and Catherine couldn't tell what he was saying. Catherine moved closer and stopped in the shade of a large elm tree.

"But sometimes a person can't wait forever," Stewart said, looking intently at Christina.

"It wouldn't be forever."

"It might as well be. Father wants to apprentice me to a distant cousin of his in London, and if nothing changes soon, then there's little to prevent me from following his wishes."

Christina sat silently for what seemed like a very long time. Stewart looked away and leaned against the fence.

Finally Christina spoke. "Stewart," she said in a solemn tone.

He turned around, sensing the importance of what she was about to say.

"I need to tell you something, something that gives me much pleasure." She paused, and he stepped toward her, hopefully. "And," she continued, "something that gives me much pain. I'll be going to Zion, to America, in a little more than a month's time."

"What?" he almost shouted.

"Yes," she said, trying to keep her voice steady.

"But, Christina, what about the two of us? What about the future?"

"It is the future that draws me, Stewart. If it weren't for the future I would stay right here, for here is my home. And the possibility of our being together would almost certainly bring me happiness."

"But then . . ."

She held up her hand, preventing him from speaking. "I've made up my mind. It's the right thing to do. I need to join my family. I must take Joan."

"But couldn't you come back?"

"I cannot promise anything, Stewart. It would be so long. And chances are you'd be in London, and there would by then be someone else who would hold your heart."

"Someone else?" he said unbelievingly. "How could there ever be someone else?"

Christina made no reply.

There was a heavy silence. Stewart looked down at the ground and kicked at a small rock. Suddenly he looked up, his eyes wide and shining triumphantly.

"And the money for passage? How could you possibly have arranged enough?" he asked. "Why, just a fortnight ago you were lamenting that you might never see your family again and that this blessed Zion of yours would remain only a dream."

Now it was Christina's turn to look at the ground. "There is a way, a way that has just recently opened up."

"And?" he asked, pressing her for an answer.

"There was a man, a musician, passing through this way last week. I asked him about the worth of my violin, and he said he would give me enough to book passage to America for me and Joan, with some left over in case we need it on our way."

"Your violin?" he asked incredulously.

She nodded, not trusting herself to speak.

"But, Christina, you can't be serious!"

"I must get to Zion," Christina said, her voice filled with determination.

"Is it worth your violin?" Stewart asked, still unable to comprehend.

Christina looked straight at him. "Yes."

"Christina, that is like your very soul," Stewart said softly, looking intently at her for what seemed a very long time. Then he turned around and began walking away. "I'll be back. You stay right here," he said. "I'll be gone but just a moment." And with that, he began running.

Catherine thought of staying hidden, but Christina looked so forlorn and disheartened that she stepped forward. "Christina?" she said timidly, hoping her intrusion would be forgiven.

Christina looked up, attempting a smile. There was a long silence. Finally Catherine spoke. "It's hard to think of you selling the violin."

"I'm afraid it's the only way. And even the dearest of things are not as important as those that last forever, like families."

"But it was made by family."

"I know," said Christina ruefully. "But I must get to

America, and I can think of no other way. People have been kind to let me help them, but in the months I've been here I've only managed to save a little less than half of what is needed for my passage alone. At that rate it would be almost four years before we would be able to leave, and I can't wait that long, Catherine, not when there's a way to leave sooner. Even if it involves a sacrifice."

Catherine could only nod her head in understanding.

They sat together for a long while, and Catherine could hear the sound of birds in the trees and feel the sunlight on her arms. There was a cool breeze. It was very peaceful, but inwardly Catherine could sense Christina's turmoil. She knew how Christina felt about the violin and about Stewart and her family and the gospel. How difficult it seemed that all those things didn't work together, that each of them tugged and pulled their separate ways inside her great-great-great-grandmother's heart.

Catherine heard the sound of footsteps on the road behind her. She turned and saw Stewart running towards them. His hair flew back, and she could tell by his red face that he had been running for quite some distance.

Christina stood and faced him as he approached. Stewart stopped short, bent over, and took a number of deep breaths. Even before he said a word he held out a small leather pouch. "Here," he finally managed.

Christina took the pouch and hefted it. Slowly, she opened the top and looked in. Then quickly she closed it and held it out toward Stewart.

He backed up several steps. "I will not take it back, not ever," he said defiantly. Then, softening his voice, he added, "It's for you."

"But, Stewart, you know I could never accept this."

"And why not?"

"It's just not right."

"It's enough to get you to America, to your Zion, and you won't have to sell your violin."

"Stewart—," she began, but was interrupted.

"Christina," he said seriously, "I know how deeply you love this land and this violin. If going to be with your family in what you call a promised land means that much to you, then that is what I want you to do, and I want to help you. I want you to be happy," he said more softly, "because I love you."

"But, Stewart!"

"Christina, there are many things I've hoped and dreamed for us, but you've never seemed to share those dreams. Please don't take away the pleasure of my giving you this money. The thought of your happiness will bring me peace when you have gone away and I am off to London learning a trade, hoping that someday you might return."

Christina reached out and put her arms around him. "Thank you," she said, tears running down her cheeks. "Thank you."

Stewart stepped back, and Catherine could see that he was trying to hold back his tears. He stepped forward quickly, kissed Christina on the cheek, then turned and walked quickly away.

Christina held the bag of money to her closely and, with tears streaming down her face, watched him walk away.

Chapter Twelve

"Catherine, you're going to be late if you don't hurry!" Her mother's voice came up the stairwell with a hint of impatience.

"I'm hurrying," Catherine said, brushing through her hair again and again. *I don't know why I'm so nervous tonight,* she wondered to herself. *It's not like I've never played the violin in a recital before.*

She held the curling iron steady, getting her bangs just right.

"Ouch," she cried out as the curling iron rested against her forehead. She jerked it away instantly, then looked in the mirror. The damage had been done. There, right in the middle of her forehead, was a small red mark. She felt like screaming as she sat down on the edge of the bathtub.

"Catherine, you're going to be late."

"I'm not going!" she shouted.

"Yes you are. Now, hurry up."

"I'm not going."

She could hear her mother coming up the stairs.

"What's the matter?"

"I burned myself with the curling iron. I hate the dumb thing."

"Here, let me see," her mother said kindly.

Catherine pulled back her bangs.

"You do seem a little hotheaded tonight," her mother said, smiling.

Catherine made another face, then laughed in spite of herself. "Sometimes you are a little funny, Mother."

"True, true," her mother said, flattered. "But I'm not as little as I used to be."

Catherine groaned. "Maybe I'd better take that back."

Her mother smiled. "It wouldn't do you any good. Now, get your sweater and hustle downstairs. You look great. Just make sure your bangs are combed down over your forehead."

Catherine hurried into the junior high auditorium where the recital would be held and unpacked her violin. Most of the other students were already there warming up.

"It's about time you got here," Jackie Maher whispered. "Mr. Hardcastle was looking for you."

Catherine forced a smile. "Well, here I am." Immediately she felt bad for using what her mother would call "a rather snotty tone of voice." Tuning her instrument, Catherine tried to forget how annoyed she was with Jackie. Instead, she tried to concentrate on the pieces she would be playing and made sure her music was all there.

Then, just minutes later, Mr. Hardcastle stepped to the microphone and in a rather dramatic tone began. "Ladies and gentlemen, parents and grandparents, brothers and sisters of the performers, we welcome you to our annual summer recital this evening. We would ask that you refrain from talking during the performance. If any of you have brought some young music lovers with you who may cause a disturbance, we would invite you to go to room 16, which is just down the hall to your left. There the recital can be heard over the school's sound system. Thank you for your attendance and your support of our budding musicians. And now, without further ado, we will follow the printed program."

Catherine gradually relaxed, and by the time it was her turn she had become absorbed in the music. She played her solo pieces with relaxed intensity, letting the bow rise and fall across the strings and feeling herself caught up in the emotion of the pieces. For a few seconds she even thought of Christina and how obvious it was that she enjoyed playing the violin. Then the music took over again, and Catherine floated along with the melodies.

Then it was time for the piece she was least looking forward to. Mr. Hardcastle had talked her into playing in a violin trio with Amy Shumway and Jackie Maher. They had practiced only twice together, and Catherine was not thrilled, for several reasons, to be playing. Besides, Jackie had this way of looking at her with undisguised disgust if she made any type of mistake, while Jackie herself had the great ability not to even notice her own wrong notes.

The first two movements of the piece went quite well, and Catherine was surprised and pleased.

Then it happened. She heard a sharp *twing* next to her. Jackie Maher's E string had broken. It so surprised Jackie that she played several notes completely out of tune. Mr. Czerny, their teacher at school, had tried to teach them just to keep on going and play the notes on the A string if possible. "True musicians do not let such things lessen the quality of a performance," he had said time and time again.

But this time there was a lessening of the quality of the performance. Catherine glanced quickly over at Jackie, whose face had gone white, then bright red with embarrassment. Then, much to Catherine's surprise, Jackie said quite loudly and very plainly, "Oh, chicken feathers!"

It seemed like a very odd thing for Jackie to say, and Catherine started to laugh and hit several wrong notes herself. Then she could feel the laughter coming from Amy Shumway, and then from other musicians seated on the front row. Catherine tried to stop but it was, she could tell, time for the giggles, and there was nothing she could do to stop them. Soon there were tears running down her cheeks. The whole audience was having a hard time not bursting into the giggles. And all the while Jackie sat next to her, her jaw clenched tightly together, gripping her violin until Catherine was afraid it would break. Finally, Mr. Hardcastle stood up and tapped on the music stand.

As Mr. Hardcastle walked sternly to the microphone the laughter gradually died down, except for Catherine's; she couldn't stop. She felt herself turning red, and she got up and walked quickly behind the curtains.

Mr. Hardcastle rapped the microphone stand three times with his baton, waiting for the audience to calm down.

"Oh, chicken feathers," called out one of the boys sitting on the second row off to the side. Again laughter swept through the auditorium, and it took about twelve raps on the microphone stand for Mr. Hardcastle to finally calm everyone down.

"Due to unforeseen circumstances," he said, with as much dignity as possible, "we will take our intermission now, one number sooner than planned. The recital will continue in fifteen minutes."

"It was all your fault," Jackie said, turning coldly toward Catherine as the intermission began. "If you hadn't started giggling like some third grader everything would have been fine."

Catherine felt her temperature rising and she was about to say something back when Amy Shumway interrupted. "Oh, chicken feathers, Jackie!"

The second half of the recital went without a problem. After the final applause died away, Catherine stood up, picked up her music, and began making her way across the stage to her violin case.

"Catherine."

Catherine turned around, looking to see who had called her name. *Oh great,* she thought, *Mr. Hardcastle.*

"Catherine, you played very well tonight but . . ."

Here it comes, thought Catherine, preparing herself for one of Mr. Hardcastle's lectures on being a professional.

"But your giggling really didn't help the performance."

Catherine looked down at the ground. She could feel her face going hot with embarrassment. "I know," she said. "I'm sorry."

"However," Mr. Hardcastle continued, "I really don't blame you."

Catherine looked up quickly, not quite sure she had heard correctly. There was Mr. Hardcastle, looking at her with what appeared to be a smile on his face. She smiled back and took a deep breath. *Sometimes people just surprise you,* she thought.

Feeling much better, Catherine put her violin in the case and greeted her family.

"Great job," her mother said, giving her a hug.

"Yes, you sounded excellent," added her father, patting her on the shoulder. "Especially on that last solo number you played, what's its name?"

"I learned it from a friend. It's an old English folk tune called 'Dives and Lazarus.'"

"You know, it sounded quite familiar but I can't quite put my finger on it."

"Like a hymn maybe?" asked Catherine innocently.

Her father looked thoughtful for several seconds. "Yes, like a hymn," he said finally.

"'If You Could Hie to Kolob,' number 284."

"Well, well," her father said, smiling. "Aren't we the smart one."

"That was the best recital you've done," said Tony. "My favorite part was when everyone started laughing."

"Oh, chicken feathers," said Andrew, and the family laughed together.

"Catherine?"

It was Amy Shumway and her parents.

"Are you still coming out to dinner with us?"

"Yes," she said, continuing to move down the hallway. "I even remembered to bring my money." Suddenly Catherine stopped. "My violin! I left it in the auditorium. I'll be right back," she said, hurrying back the way she had come.

Catherine opened the door and entered the auditorium. She walked carefully down the now almost darkened aisle to where she had left her violin. Suddenly she shuddered, and her stomach went cold and turned over.

There was nothing there. Stunned for just a moment, she wondered if she was looking in the right place. But, yes, it was right there that just a few minutes before she had carefully put her violin in its case.

She knelt down and looked under the seats, hoping that perhaps it had fallen. But there was nothing, and the sick feeling spread through her whole body. She sat down, feeling numb and shaky. Christina's violin, the violin Stewart had sacrificed his life savings for; Giuseppe Viotti's violin, made over two hundred years ago in Cremona, Italy—she had lost it.

She kneeled down and said a short prayer, begging her Father in Heaven to help her find it. She stood up, worrying that she hadn't enough faith. She walked slowly back to her family, who stood talking with Amy and her parents.

"What's wrong, honey?" asked her mother as she approached.

At first she could hardly say the words but finally she whispered, "My violin's gone."

"Are you sure?" her father asked.

Catherine could only nod her head.

Moments later the small group stood in the auditorium. The violin was nowhere to be seen, and they had no idea of where else to look.

"Maybe," suggested Mr. Shumway, "whoever took it went out that door up by the stage."

The despondent group moved toward the door. It opened into an empty parking lot.

They stood in silence for a few moments more.

"I suppose we'd better notify the police," Catherine's mother said.

"And call the music stores and pawn shops in town to alert them of the theft," added her father.

The group continued to stand there somberly, and Catherine could feel the beginning tears start to fall now that the shock was wearing off.

"Catherine! Catherine! Here it is! Over here!"

It was Andrew's voice coming from near a large trash bin in the corner of the parking lot. Quickly Catherine ran across the lot, then stopped. There was the case, open, and her violin lying on the asphalt nearby. Carefully she picked it up. There was a small gash about an inch long across the top, but other than that it seemed to be all right. Catherine picked up the bow, which was several feet away leaning against a chain-link fence. Quietly she played a few notes and smiled.

"I think it will be fine," she said, her voice mingling hope and relief. "It seems to play just the same. Thank you, Andrew."

Andrew smiled and put his hands in his pocket and said, "I can't figure why anyone would take the violin and then just throw it away."

Suddenly Catherine looked down and picked up the violin case. She rummaged through it for just a minute, then quickly glanced around the area. "They took my money," she said.

"What money?" asked her mother.

"The money I brought to go out to dinner with the Shumways, twenty-five dollars. It was in my violin case."

"Well," her father said, "it's a good thing the thief didn't realize the value of the violin."

Catherine took a deep breath. She was just thankful that she had the violin back. It was far more valuable to her than the thousands of dollars it would bring at the store. *How could I ever have visited Christina again, knowing I had lost the violin?*

"Well, shall we go?" asked Mr. Shumway.

Catherine hesitated.

"I can lend you the twenty-five dollars," Catherine's father offered.

"Well," Catherine said, trying to be polite.

Sensing her hesitation, Amy's mother spoke up. "I think maybe we've had enough excitement for one night. What if we go out Saturday evening instead?"

"That would be great," Catherine said gratefully.

"And it will give Catherine time to earn that twenty-five dollars again," said her father with a grin.

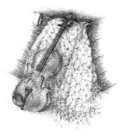

Chapter Thirteen

Catherine undid the latch, then opened her bedroom window and looked out into the backyard. The leaves on the trees were dark green and full, and the grass was trimmed and vibrant. In the corner of the yard was a cluster of petunias. Their bright pink and purple colors brought Catherine a deep sense of enjoyment. Catherine sat in the window sill for several minutes, breathing in the summer air. Everything seemed to be especially bright and enjoyable.

Catherine jumped down from the window sill, put the shawl around her shoulders, and said quietly, "Christina Cooper, August 15, 1841." She repeated the same thing twice more and watched as the now familiar shimmering in the air took place.

Before the air had even cleared she felt a wave of nausea as a terrible smell filled her nostrils. Liverpool! Catherine put her hand up to her face and covered her mouth and nose. It didn't help much. Gradually her eyes adjusted to the light. There, all around her, were dozens of people lying on the floor, wrapped in tattered blankets. Some lay in what seemed to be small wooden bunk beds. The sounds of people coughing and moaning gave her a creepy feeling, and it was hard to stand as she kept tipping from side to side. Suddenly realizing she was on a ship, she grabbed hold of a wooden post near her and looked for Christina.

At least they made it aboard a ship, she thought as she looked around. Finally she saw Joan sitting on one of the wooden berths. She had what looked to be a damp rag in her hand and was wiping someone's forehead. *Christina!* thought Catherine, and a chill went up her back. As best she could she made her way toward the two of them, stepping over bodies and baggage and buckets that smelled horrible. Catherine felt like throwing up and even thought of trying to come back on another day. *No,* she said, ashamed of herself, *how could I leave Christina in such a horrible place and in such a condition? Maybe I can be of some help.*

She knelt down as she approached and saw Christina looking pale and weak. Christina's eyes were open but they were staring straight ahead and didn't seem to be seeing anything. Catherine felt like crying.

"Christina?" she said softly. "Christina?"

"What?" came the reply. "Who is it?"

"There, there sister," said Joan. "Don't say anything. Just rest."

"Christina, it's Catherine."

"Catherine?"

"Shhh," said Joan.

"Are you all right?"

"Feeling wretched," Christina said, struggling to sit up. "Joan, help me on deck. I need some fresh air."

"But, Christina," Joan responded, "you know I can't lift you."

"I'll manage. And Catherine can help."

Joan looked around but could see no one. Catherine could tell Joan was confused, wondering if Christina was delirious.

There, all around her, were dozens of people lying
on the floor, wrapped in tattered blankets.

Using all her strength, Catherine helped as Joan lifted Christina to her feet. It took them several minutes to get to the stairs that led to the deck, but once they made it, Catherine felt much better. The ship pitched and tossed gently on the waves. Underneath the cloudy sky, the breeze, though somewhat salty, was much better than the fetid air below deck.

Christina leaned against the side of the ship. She was pale and thinner than Catherine remembered her, and she had a hard time standing up straight. Catherine shook her head and shuddered.

"Joan, see if you can find me some water, would you?" Christina asked.

"Will you be all right if I leave you?"

"Yes. Now, run along," Christina said, trying her best to smile briefly. "I'll stay right here, so you can find me."

At least she hasn't lost her sense of humor, thought Catherine.

Joan left but turned around every few steps to check on her sister, and Catherine could see the love and concern in her eyes.

"We've been on the ocean for a month now," Christina said, laboring with almost every word. Then she smiled weakly. "But at least we're on our way to Zion. There were times I thought we'd never make it."

"How long have you been sick?" Catherine asked.

"I'm not sure. It seems like a long time. I say a hundred prayers a day, and the Lord has assured me that I will see my family again. Elder Taylor promised Joan and me that we would both make it to Zion after he blessed her. And that is all I ask. I think I can last through almost anything if I know that I will finally see Mother and Father again."

"Do you ever wish you were back in England?"

Christina nodded her head. "Sometimes." She paused for several seconds. "Sometimes I even imagine what it might have been like being married to Stewart, living with him in a small, neat house in Chatburn, and how nice it would be, and how quiet and beautiful and clean it would be. But I know it was best to leave."

"I don't see how you can stay so strong."

"The only thing that brings me great pain is that, with all the excitement, I left the shawl and violin at Aunt Martha's."

"Oh, Christina!" Catherine lamented.

Christina tried to smile. "When things get really bad, and when I start to feel sorry for myself, I think about the times Elder Heber C. Kimball was in Chatburn. He had preached a number of times in our village and in several others nearby. It was at such a meeting that my father was first filled with testimony of the Restoration. He took those of us who were old enough to understand to the next meeting.

Christina stopped for a few minutes as if to relive in her mind what she was about to express to Catherine and to gather her strength before going on.

"He was much beloved of the people and always preached with the power of God. We loved him for his kindness and love for us and we were sorry that he would have to return home. I remember one afternoon in 1838 in particular. It was a beautiful day, full of sunshine and warmth. As Elder Kimball was leaving, we children followed after him for more than a mile, singing hymns and shouting praises. The older folks would come to their doorsteps or windows and call out blessings upon his head. The Spirit of the Lord was most powerful, Catherine. I have never felt the like of it again, but I can almost feel it now just talking about it.

"Elder Kimball was crying, and the people were crying. He even stopped several times to wash the tears from his cheeks in a stream of water that ran near the road. He took off his hat and knelt and prayed to God, and the whole countryside seemed filled with light and goodness. Even after he had disappeared from our sight, that feeling lingered for several hours, filling us with joy and hope and the knowledge that indeed he was a servant of the very God of Israel.

"It is that day I remember when things get most difficult, and then I know I can continue, that I can be faithful and that the Lord will bless me."

Christina looked straight ahead. "I'm feeling stronger just talking about it."

Catherine heard a voice call out, "Christina! Are you all right?"

She turned to see Joan approaching.

"I'm sorry, but this is all the water I could get," she said, handing a small cup to her sister. It was less than half full.

"That should be sufficient," Christina said, patting her sister on the head. "Thank you for looking after me, Joan. You've been as good a nurse as anybody could ask for."

Joan smiled.

Catherine could see that it would be awkward to stay, and there was really nothing else she could do. She put her arm on Christina's shoulder and gave a short wave. Christina waved back. "Thank you," she said, "for caring as well."

"You already said thank you, Christina," Joan said.

"So I did," Christina said, smiling weakly. "So I did."

"Christina?" Joan asked in a concerned voice. "Are you certain you're feeling all right?"

Christina nodded. "Much better, thank you."

Catherine smiled to herself and then, moments later, she was back in her bedroom.

An hour later when Catherine's mother came home from running errands, she was rather amazed to see Catherine leaning over the bathtub scrubbing with all the strength she could muster.

"Looks like you're doing a great job, Catherine," she said in a voice that indicated surprise. "But the bathtub isn't even your job this week."

Catherine looked up. "I know, but it's just so nice to have things clean and shiny and smelling fresh," she said, thinking back to the horrible conditions aboard the ship. "I think it makes a big difference in how we feel. Don't you think so?"

Catherine's mother nodded, then tilted her head a little to the side and gave her a quizzical look. "Yes, it certainly does make a difference. That's true."

She started to leave, then stopped in the doorway. "Maybe you ought to check the laundry room," she said, with a twinkle in her eye, "and see how you feel there."

Catherine turned around and shook her head. "Let's not get carried away with this," she said with a grin.

Chapter Fourteen

Two days later Catherine sat glumly on the swing set in the backyard. She was bored—bored and upset. She had been planning on going shopping for some new clothes, but something had come up with Andrew, and her mother wasn't able to take her. Now she was stuck home with nothing to do because Amy and some of her other friends had gone up the canyon without her when they thought she was going shopping all afternoon. Catherine took a deep breath and let it out slowly, feeling sorry for herself.

Then, remembering she hadn't watered her plants for over a week, Catherine got up, kicked at a soccer ball lying on the grass, and walked back into the house.

Moments later she finished watering the plants in her room. She looked around the room and counted them. Seventeen. Usually her plants helped cheer her up, but not this time. She needed something that would help her relax and get in a good mood. She thought of the shawl.

Catherine pulled her bedroom door shut. She opened her top drawer, took out the shawl, wrapped it around her, and sat down in her window seat. The shawl felt warm and reassuring, and gradually Catherine relaxed. Her mind drifted off her own problems, and she thought of Christina, who had been sick on the ship when she had last visited her. *I wonder how she and Joan are doing now,* Catherine thought to herself, knowing there was only one way to find out.

Catherine pulled the shawl a little tighter around her and spoke out loud, "Christina Cooper, August 25, 1841, Christina Cooper, August 25, 1841, Christina Cooper, August 25, 1841." The air shimmered and her familiar surroundings disappeared.

She lurched forward and fell hard on the wooden deck. She tried to get up, but the ship pitched again, sending her sprawling. Then a wave hit the ship from the side, drenching her with cold seawater. Stunned, Catherine shook her head slightly to clear her thoughts. She shivered and stayed down on her hands and knees and looked around. About thirty feet away she could see Christina holding on to some of the rigging. She was wet too and was struggling to keep from falling. Then, almost by magic, the ocean began to calm, the waves diminished, and the ship steadied, although the sky above them was still filled with dark and lowering clouds. The two of them moved quickly toward each other.

"Christina!" she called out. "Are you all right?"

Christina nodded.

"Are you feeling better?" Catherine asked, looking closely at Christina's thin face and pale complexion. "Or are you still sick?"

"Better, I think," Christina said softly. "But for most of the last two weeks I have been unable to get up and I haven't been able to eat hardly anything."

"That doesn't really sound to me like you're much better," said Catherine, noticing how thin and haggard Christina looked. "And what about Joan, how is she doing?"

"Joan is well. She hasn't been sick one moment since the Apostle gave her that blessing."

"Have you had a blessing?"

Christina nodded. "And I know it has helped, at least somewhat. Maybe I don't have the faith I need to be healed completely."

"I wish I had half your faith."

Just then a loud crack of thunder boomed above them and seemed to send shock waves through the air. Large, dark clouds came swirling toward the ship, and the wind suddenly gusted strongly again.

"We'd better go below as quickly as we can," said Christina, grabbing Catherine by the arm.

A number of passengers were already crowding around the hold trying to get below at the same time. The wind hurled itself against the waves and sent a spray of water across the deck, dowsing Catherine and Christina once again. Catherine shivered as, finally, they were able to get below. Again the stench and feeling of sickness filled Catherine's nostrils. It had been so easy to forget all this once she had returned home the last time.

"Joan? Joan?" Christina called as they stumbled toward the far side of the ship.

"I'm over here, Christina," her sister called back. She was lying on one of the smaller berths.

"I didn't think you had two berths of your own," Catherine said.

"We didn't," Christina said, hesitating. "The other one belonged to some Saints from Liverpool. But three of the family died last week and were buried at sea. That little boy over there, David," she said, pointing beyond Joan to the edge of the berth where a little dark-haired boy who looked about Tony's age lay curled up on the blankets, "is the only one of the family left. We're taking him to Zion with us."

Catherine swallowed hard. She shook her head in disbelief.

"It's been hard," Christina said.

"Has . . . ," Catherine began, and then she paused and whispered, "has anyone else died?"

"One other. A baby, just four months old, died just a few days ago. Her mother is right over there," Christina said, pointing toward the back of the ship.

"She doesn't look well," Catherine said.

"She's not," returned Christina, shaking her head.

"When do you reach America?"

"They say it will be almost two weeks from now."

"I don't see how you can live another day here in all this filth and with all these people sick and everything."

"We try not to even think about it. We have a hope for the future. We live with a hope that Zion will be peaceful and clean, that it will be worth everything we've had to go through to get there. But," Christina added, "there are some who are not Saints, who laugh at us, call us dreamers and worshippers of Joe Smith."

"But we don't worship Joseph Smith, we worship Jesus."

"I know."

"But Joseph is a true prophet."

Christina smiled. "I'm already converted, remember? And I'm very anxious to see him."

Catherine relaxed, smiled, and nodded. "I know."

The ship pitched and rolled, and another ferocious clap of thunder rang above them. The small boy on the berth lay without moving. He held a torn blanket to his chin and began to whimper.

"It's been awfully hard for him since his parents died, and whenever there's a storm he frets until it's over. I'd best go tend to him for a little while."

Catherine sat watching for nearly an hour, listening

to the storm rage around the ship. By the time the wind stopped and the waves calmed, Catherine was feeling a bit nauseated.

Finally both the young boy and Christina had fallen asleep.

"Good-bye, Christina," she whispered softly. "And may the Lord be with you."

Christina stirred slightly but did not wake up.

Moments later Catherine stood again in her room and once again breathed deeply of the fresh air, feeling grateful for a clean room. She sat on the edge of her bed. How soft and comfortable it felt, and how good it would feel to snuggle under the covers and fall asleep in a nice warm house!

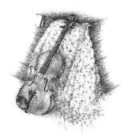

Chapter Fifteen

Catherine felt the force of gravity pull her deeper into the seat of the silver 747. She looked out the window and felt the nose of the plane tilting upward. Gradually the plane rose into the air, and the cars, buildings, and roadways got smaller and smaller beneath her. Moments later the plane leveled off and all she could see were the snow covered mountains east of Salt Lake City. It was Catherine's first ever ride in an airplane, and she shivered slightly as she stared down thousands of feet to the ground, feeling a little apprehensive about being so high in the air.

She looked over at her father, who was leaning back, resting with his eyes closed. In the last few years he had started to travel quite a bit, ever since he and a few business partners had started some type of computer software company. Catherine wasn't exactly sure what the software did or what the training was all about except that it had something to do with the medical profession. But she knew her father enjoyed his work and she also knew that he tried to keep his travel to a minimum. Still, two or three times a month he had to fly somewhere to help with some software training or solve some problem that had come up.

It had been only ten days before that her father had announced at the dinner table that he had to fly to New Orleans for two days.

"New Orleans?" Catherine had responded excitedly. "I'd love to go to New Orleans."

"Why's that?" her father had asked.

"Well," she replied, "it just sounds fun, and besides, didn't the Coopers land in New Orleans on their way to Nauvoo?"

"Why wouldn't they just sail to New York or something?" asked Tony. "I thought everyone had to sail past the Statue of Liberty if they came to America from another country."

"You've certainly taken a rather extraordinary interest in the William Cooper family, Catherine," her mother said, smiling and shaking her head in amazement. "I imagine you'll be excited to meet them in the next world."

Catherine nodded her head. "I'm sure I will."

Then, later that night, as Catherine was getting ready for bed, there had come a knock on her bedroom door.

"Come in," she said, looking up from a book she was reading.

Her father slowly pushed open the door. "Do you have a few minutes?"

"Sure."

He came over and sat on the edge of the bed. "So, the Coopers landed in New Orleans, did they?"

"Yes."

"And when was that?"

"In the 1840s."

"I suppose New Orleans would have changed quite a bit in over a hundred and fifty years."

Catherine nodded her head. "I'm sure it has."

Her father just nodded his head and smiled the smile he used when he was trying to be clever.

"How's the violin coming?" he asked, changing the subject.

"Fine," she replied, trying to figure out what in the world her father was getting at.

"Do you think you could survive for a few days without practicing?"

"I don't know," she said slowly. "I guess I could," she added, still wondering what was going on. "Although, Mr. Hardcastle just gave me a couple of new fiddle pieces that he wants us to use in a competition coming up, and I don't want to be the last one to learn them."

"Well, I guess you'd probably better work on those pieces. I don't imagine that you'd like to see how much New Orleans has changed in the last one hundred and fifty years anyway."

Catherine looked at her father with a quizzical expression. "What do you mean?" she asked, half beginning to hope.

"I mean, how would you like to go to New Orleans with me for a couple of days?"

Catherine had let out a whoop of joy, sat up, and given her father a hug.

Catherine leaned back against the headrest, took a sip of root beer from the small plastic glass the flight attendant had brought her, and closed her eyes for just a moment. Her thoughts went to Christina. How different her few hours' flight across the country was from her ancestor's ocean voyage of several weeks, with a hard, wooden bunk, a few blankets, little food, and conditions that were dirty and horrible smelling. *Here I am, flying through the air at hundreds of miles per hour, sitting in a clean, soft seat, and having someone check on me every little while to see if everything is all right or if I need a pillow or would like something to drink. If Christina could see me, it might be hard for her to understand.*

Catherine heard a sharp crackling noise over the intercom, then heard the Captain's voice. "We'll be arriving in New Orleans in less than ten minutes now. Those of you on the left side of the plane will have a magnificent view as we begin our descent and circle toward our landing. As you can see, the weather is clear, sunny, and about 84 degrees, with a slight breeze out of the southeast. A very nice welcome to the Old South. So, just sit back and relax. We'll have you safely on the ground in the Crescent City in just a matter of minutes."

Catherine sat up and looked out the window. In the distance she could see the Mississippi River. It was huge! She had never seen anything like it in her life. And she could see the sprawling city of New Orleans, even bigger than she had pictured it. The downtown skyscrapers shone brightly in the sun of early afternoon.

"Quite a city," her father said, leaning over to take a look as well.

"Have you been here before?"

"A couple of times," her father replied. "I wish we had more time to take you around to see some things. It's going to be a short trip, but I think we'll have a few minutes this afternoon and maybe a couple of free hours tomorrow."

All at once Catherine sensed the plane drop slightly, and her stomach felt hollow. Suddenly the ground seemed to rush up to meet them, and moments later she felt the wheels touch the tarmack, heard the sound of air whooshing past the plane, and gradually felt the plane slow to a halt.

After dropping off their baggage at the hotel, Catherine's father looked at his watch. "I don't have my first meeting for almost two hours. What if we went to see a few things?"

"Sure."

Ten minutes later the two of them were in the famous French Quarter of the city, walking down Canal Street, a very wide road with department stores and specialty shops on either side.

"It's over half a football field from one side of the road to the other," her father said as they walked down the street toward the Mississippi River. He stopped and pointed at a tall building a little to their right. "That's the International Trade Mart—thirty-three stories high with an observation tower on top. I thought you might like to see what the city looked like from up there."

Catherine nodded. "That'd be great."

Her father looked down at his watch. "I think we have time," he said. "At least that will give you an idea of the city. Then maybe tomorrow you could choose a couple of places to go that seem to be the most interesting to you."

"Sounds good to me," Catherine responded.

Moments later they were moving rapidly up the elevator, then on to the observation deck thirty-three stories into the air. From the top Catherine stared down at the Mississippi that stretched out below. She followed its course for as far as she could see. She thought of Christina coming up the river on a ship, of how excited she must have been to finally arrive in America. Catherine couldn't imagine how it would be not to see your

105

family for so long, not being able to call them on the telephone, and only being able to receive a few letters over a period of many months.

She turned the other way and saw the city of New Orleans laid out in front of her. "What's that, over there?" she asked, pointing to a huge, white-topped dome several blocks away.

"The Superdome," her father replied. "You know, where they hold sports events, conventions, and trade shows."

"It's a big place."

"All this area is called the French Quarter. It's famous for jazz, nightclubs, antique shops, and restaurants, one of which we'll go to tonight when I get done with my meetings."

"Sounds great!" said Catherine, smiling, even though she had eaten enough pop and peanuts on the airplane to last her several hours.

"And down there, below us," her father said, pointing a little to the left, "are the docks. They still have ocean-going vessels come in here loaded with all kinds of things."

"Is that where the docks were a hundred and fifty years ago?" Catherine asked excitedly. "Would it be the same place that the Coopers landed?"

"I'm not sure," her father responded. "But I imagine so. I guess we could ask."

"Do they still have passenger ships come in?"

"I think so."

"That's one of the places I'd really like to visit tomorrow."

"I might have guessed," said her father, laughing.

On the way down, the elevator went so quickly Catherine felt her stomach drop. *What would Christina think about elevators and skyscrapers, airplanes and huge ocean liners?* she wondered, remembering again the horrible conditions aboard the ship.

Several hours later Catherine sat alone in their hotel room. She stood up and walked over to the door. It was securely locked. She felt a little apprehensive sitting alone in the room by herself in a big city so far away from home. And her father wouldn't be back to the hotel until a little after seven o'clock. That was almost three hours away.

"This is a very safe hotel," her father had said, "but keep the door locked and don't let anyone in for any reason. And here's the number at the front desk. If there seems to be any trouble, call and ask for Manny."

"Manny?"

"Yes. And don't worry," he added, smiling. "I'll be back as soon as I can, and then you'll be in for a treat that will send your tastebuds into orbit."

"Dad," she had replied, shaking her head, "you come up with some of the corniest phrases sometimes."

Her father had laughed, given her a quick hug, and then left.

She walked to the window and looked out across the city spreading miles into the distance. She thought of the thousands upon ,thousands of people living and working out there. And she didn't know any of them. All of a sudden she had the urge to pray. She kneeled down by the window. "Father in Heaven," she began. "Please bless my father that things will go well for him and that he might return safely and that I will be watched over and protected here. Please help me to feel safe and to feel thy Spirit. Please bless Mom and everyone at home. And I thank thee for this opportunity and for my wonderful ancestors and all they went through."

She closed in the name of Jesus Christ and stood up, feeling much calmer.

She walked back across the room and opened her suitcase. There was the shawl, folded neatly in the corner of one side. She had brought it with her just in case. Catherine picked it up and her thoughts went back to Christina. Maybe if she guessed right she could go back to when they arrived in New Orleans and see how the city looked over a hundred and fifty years earlier. *Let's see,* she thought, *I visited last on August 25. Maybe I'll try just one week later, or maybe two weeks would be better. It seemed like the journey was always taking longer than anyone thought.*

"Christina Cooper, September 7, 1841," she said three times slowly and distinctly. Again the air began to wrinkle, and Catherine's heartbeat quickened in anticipation.

Chapter Sixteen

Shouts of "Fire! Fire!" greeted Catherine as the air around her settled into a smoky haze. As her vision cleared she could see the swirling orange yellow of flames to her left.

Dozens of people ran past Catherine, scattering this way and that. Bewildered, Catherine looked quickly to see if she could find Christina. There she was, about twenty feet beyond Catherine, near the stairs that led from the deck to the hold below.

"Joan, Joan!" she was screaming as she held the hand of the small boy they had taken in. He was crying and clinging to her skirts.

"Joan!" she called out again. "Where are you?"

Catherine moved toward her, when suddenly a huge wall of flames burst with great intensity to the side of her. She jumped to the side and ran toward Christina. Catherine was just a few feet away when Christina spotted Joan near the side of the ship. Quickly Christina ran toward Joan, dragging the small boy behind her. Catherine followed after her, feeling the heat of the flames that were now burning out of control. Like a nightmare, the crackling flames reached into the sky. Shouting and screaming passengers ran this way and that in a panic as the crew hastily drew buckets of water and hurled the liquid at the onrushing fire.

Suddenly someone shouted, "Overboard! Our only chance is overboard!" And with that, he leaped into the darkness. Others followed.

"Christina!" Catherine yelled, feeling the heat of the fire drawing nearer. She turned around. There was nowhere to go. Flames had cut her off from the rest of the ship's deck; and from where she stood, Catherine couldn't see anything but flames.

She turned once more, just in time to see Christina pull Joan up by the hand to the side of the ship and grab the small ten-year-old boy in the other. She poised momentarily on the side of the ship.

"Christina!" Catherine called loudly into the firelit darkness.

Christina turned, her eyes focusing momentarily on Catherine; then she was gone over the side, pulling the other two with her.

Catherine hesitated for only an instant, then ran toward the side of the ship. Reaching out and grabbing the ship's railing at full speed, she catapulted herself over the side and felt herself falling for what seemed like forever.

Suddenly she slammed hard against the cold water of the Mississippi River and disappeared under its surface. Fighting for air, she flailed upwards as quickly as she could. She felt her head break through the surface of the water and gasped for air.

The shawl! Turning this way and that, she searched frantically, reaching into the dark waters around her. *O Father in Heaven,* she prayed, *please help me find that shawl.* She groped in the water for several more seconds. Then her left leg brushed against something, and she reached down and pulled the dripping shawl tightly to her. She took a deep breath.

Relax, she tried to tell herself, *relax.* Some of the simple things she had taught the students in her summer swimming classes, like how to tread water and how to float, now seemed extremely serious. Gradually her eyes adjusted to the darkness, and she could see parts of the burning masts toppling towards her. Paddling backwards as fast as she could she was able to avoid the burning timbers. She continued to splash and kick her way farther and farther from the ship. Her arms were beginning to hurt, and she found it hard to breathe.

"Catherine!"

She turned around as best she could. It was Christina, holding on to a piece of the ship's railing with one hand and to Joan's arm with the other. Catherine's heart skipped a beat and her stomach went cold. Where was the dark-haired boy? She looked around wildly, turning this way and that, then turned back to Christina.

"And the boy?" she shouted over the small waves that lapped around them.

"Here," Christina called back, motioning with her head behind her. It was then that Catherine saw the dark, matted-down hair of the ten-year-old as he clung to the piece of wood.

Catherine swam slowly towards the other three, keeping the shawl tightly around her. Then, just as she reached out to touch the wooden railing next to Christina, her foot touched the river bottom. Moments later she saw Christina pulled from the water by a man and pushed toward the shore where several women wrapped her in a blanket. Then it was Joan's and the young boy's turn. Catherine struggled by herself to the shore and lay down, gasping for air, her side aching from lack of oxygen.

A short while later she sat up slowly, clutching the shawl, and looked around. There was no one nearby. She felt a wave of nervousness pass through her and she shivered from the cold. *Why didn't they take me with them?* she wondered to herself. Then she remembered. No one but Christina could even see her.

She stood up and looked around in the darkness. She felt afraid. *Although,* she thought, *that's silly, if no one can see me.* She started to walk forward, hoping to find some trail to follow that would allow her to find the others. She walked for almost ten minutes and could see nothing but darkness. The wind turned colder and the wet shawl only added to her discomfort.

Well, she thought to herself, *I'll have to try and find them another time.* And with that, she pronounced her own name three times and moments later was back in the hotel room in New Orleans.

She sat down on the bed, and even though it was summer, she pulled a blanket over her. It felt so good to be warm and dry. She lay there and thought of Christina and Joan. They had not been able to escape the cold and the wet so easily. They had had to get warm and dry somehow. Would they be all right? she wondered.

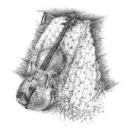

Chapter Seventeen

Late that night Catherine lay in bed, so full of shrimp and lobster and other delicious seafood she could hardly roll over. She was thinking of Christina, wondering if she had made it to New Orleans and on to Nauvoo. *In the morning,* she decided, *when Dad has to go to more meetings, I'll see if she made it safely.*

The next morning Catherine and her father walked down to the docks. The wide stretch of water would have looked very similar to Christina, Catherine thought as she stood on the docks watching the river slap against the bank.

"I wonder if our descendants will visit places we've been and wonder about what we did and what we were like," Catherine mused as she walked along the dock with her father.

"I imagine they will," he replied.

"That seems sort of strange."

"Yes, it does," said her father in a kind of faraway voice. "It might prove interesting if we could look into the future and see who was looking into the past to see us."

"Now, that's a bit confusing," Catherine said, laughing.

Her father laughed too. "I suppose so. Well, we'd better be getting back to the hotel. I have one more short meeting, then we need to check out and head back to the airport for the flight home."

Catherine felt the wind against her face as she settled once more into the past. Glancing around, she could tell she was on a riverboat, heading up what she correctly assumed was the Mississippi River. It was amazingly wide, and both sides were lined with woods. The blue sky was bright, with only a few clouds drifting to the west, and the sunlight danced on the water's surface. For a moment she was so caught up in the beauty of the surroundings she forgot to look for Christina.

Then, feeling a little embarrassed, she looked quickly around her. There, on the lower deck, she could see Christina, Joan, and David. They were in a rather large group of people that Catherine guessed were the Saints on board. She called out but realized that she would never be heard above the wind and the noise of the boat and the water. She was just about to go down the stairs when a loud shout went up from the crowd of Saints on the lower deck. Christina looked up as the ship rounded a bend in the river.

Nauvoo! There it was—bright and shining in the afternoon sun, a welcome pattern of houses, buildings, and fields tucked against the hillside upon which stood the rising foundations of the Nauvoo Temple. Catherine felt goosebumps of excitement, reverence, and awe race up and down her arms, and her heartbeat quickened.

She looked down at Christina, who stood motionless, her eyes riveted on the scene before her. There were tears running down Christina's cheeks, and she made no effort to wipe them away. Catherine felt a

Nauvoo! There it was—bright and shining in the afternoon sun. Catherine felt goosebumps of excitement, reverence, and awe race up and down her arms.

surge of love and appreciation flame within her. *What a blessing to have a great-great-great grandmother like that!*

Suddenly she saw Christina move quickly to the edge of the railing and look intently toward the shore. Then, like a child, she began jumping up and down, up and down, waving and calling out.

"Father! Father! Mother!" she called out.

Catherine looked toward the shore, peering intently at the gathering crowd of Saints.

Yes, there was William Cooper, his wife, Lavina, and the children: James, Jeremiah, and Oliver. William had his hat off and was waving it ecstatically. Catherine felt the tears begin to flow from her own eyes. She had intended to talk with Christina, tell her how much she admired and appreciated her and how glad she was that she had arrived safely, but now, as the riverboat coasted in toward the shore, she was content to watch.

Moments later the gangplank was lowered, and the crowd of Saints hurried across it to the arms of waiting friends and relatives on the shore. Catherine followed at a distance, then stopped and watched as Christina ran as quickly as she could, dragging Joan and David, toward her parents. The last fifty feet she let go of their hands and ran into the open arms of her mother and father. They hugged for what seemed like forever.

Catherine moved close enough to see the joyful, tear-stained faces of her ancestors and to feel their great relief and gratitude. She was not close enough to hear what they said, but she could well imagine. Then she saw William Cooper draw his family to one side. They knelt as a group, and she could tell that he was praying to the Lord, a prayer of thanksgiving for the reuniting of his family. She felt a sudden lump in her throat, hurting so bad she could hardly swallow. *Why should happiness hurt so much?* she wondered. She took a deep breath and brushed away her tears. She looked again. It was a scene she would remember for a long, long time. *Well, she thought, this really isn't the time to intrude.* She took one last look and waved her hand slowly in a gesture of good-bye.

That afternoon Catherine felt a tingling of excitement inside as the plane taxied up to the gate. She was impatient as the passengers in front of her took their luggage from the overhead bins and slowly filed out in front of her.

Moments later she and her father were making their way quickly up the walkway. There was her mother, and Tony and Andrew, and Adrienne and Audrey.

"Mom! Mom!" Catherine called out.

Her mother turned and smiled. "Catherine," she called back, then hurried towards her, her arms outstretched. Catherine felt all her mother's love in that hug. "Glad to have you back," she said quietly, with a catch in her voice.

Catherine felt tears fill her eyes. "It's good to be back," she said softly.

For just a moment her mind went back to Christina and her family at Nauvoo. No wonder the Cooper reunion had left them almost speechless with joy. *There's something about a family,* Catherine thought, watching her brothers and sisters clustered around as her mother and father greeted each other with a hug and a kiss, *something safe and deep and good.*

Afterword

Although the Church history portions of this book are based loosely on real events, nearly all the specific events in this book are fictional. For instance, many of the British Saints did sail from Liverpool, England, but a ship named *New Hope* never actually sailed from Liverpool. Also, while many of the difficulties with sickness and cramped quarters aboard the ship are based on real accounts, the fire aboard the ship as it neared New Orleans is fictional.